Sally's
Bones

MacKenzie Cadenhead
Illustrated by T.S. Spookytooth

Cover design by Liz Demeter/Demeter Design
Cover images © MightyIsland/iStockphoto.com; jammydesign/iStockphoto.com

The characters and events portrayed in this book are fictitious or are used fictitiously. Any similarity to real persons, living or dead, is purely coincidental and not intended by the author.

Published by Sourcebooks Jabberwocky, an imprint of Sourcebooks, Inc.
P.O. Box 4410, Naperville, Illinois 60567-4410
(630) 961-3900
Fax: (630) 961-2168
www.jabberwockykids.com

Library of Congress Cataloging-in-Publication data is on file with the publisher.

Source of Production: Webcom, Toronto, Ontario, Canada
Date of Production: August 2011
Run Number: 15766

Printed and bound in Canada.
WC 10 9 8 7 6 5 4 3 2 1

To Dan and Smudge

Prologue

Sally Simplesmith was determined not to vomit. Though she had never been a fan of recess, looking at the schoolyard as it was now—turned into a makeshift courtroom for the trial of her best friend—she longed for the days of being picked last in kickball. Standing beside the milk-crate witness box, she scanned the scene before her. Officer Stu banged his gavel repeatedly as he shouted, in vain, for order. The evil Dog Catcher turned red and screamed for an immediate judgment. Her father, unable to look her in the eye after his shocking betrayal, nervously pinched his thumbs. The audience of bloodthirsty neighbors and maniac mutts howled cruelties at her and the accused from behind the jungle gym gallery. Sally wanted to be surprised by how quickly their adoration had turned to anger, but she wasn't. Part of her had expected this all along.

She looked, then, at her best friend, Bones, so small and helpless, boxed in by half a dozen milk crates. He tilted his head and gazed up at her with empty black eyes.

She reached out her hand to him. He leaned in and gave it a single lick.

The wind wailed in the trees, nearly matching the cries of the angry mob in pitch and volume. The sound reminded Sally of that night in the graveyard when she'd first found Bones. She recalled her fear, her desperation, and finally her joy at the miraculous gift that the spirit of her mother had given her—a new best friend who would change her life forever.

Out of the corner of her eye, Sally saw the first enraged civilian break the chalk-drawn line that separated the spectators from those involved in the court's proceedings. It wouldn't be long before others followed, and she knew exactly for whom they would come.

Inhaling deeply, Sally filled her lungs with resolve. Though she would never exactly remember her next few steps, more than one witness could have sworn they heard the petite raven-haired girl whisper to the trees: "Give. Me. Death."

Chapter 1

2 Months, 28 Days, 9 Hours, and 12 Minutes Earlier...

The morning before Sally Simplesmith came face-to-face with death, she made the acquaintance of pure evil. Leaning awkwardly against the gate of the Vanderperfect Estate, Sally chewed on her fingernails, trying desperately not to get too excited about the impending arrival of the only friend she had ever had.

Sally was not a popular girl. To suggest that she had few friends would be untrue. To say that she had none would be more technically correct. For one thing, Sally looked nothing like the other girls at Merryland Middle School. With her blunt-bobbed hair, black as a starless night, and her chalky white skin, Sally clashed with the rosy blonds and olive-toned brunettes that surrounded her. While they preferred coordinated

sweater sets and perfectly tailored dresses, Sally found satisfaction in worn-in blue jeans and a rotation of concert T-shirts featuring her favorite band, Tone Death.

"*Dead Ringers?*" Chati Chattercathy once asked about the text of a particularly distressing T-shirt. It featured an image of identical twin girls hitting each other with their cell phones. "I think your shirt might be a bit too aggressive for acceptable school attire, don't you?" the almond-eyed beauty kindly offered. "Also, I don't get it."

Encouraged by her classmate's interest, Sally explained: "Oh no, it's okay. It's a Tone Death song that's less about violence than it is about how our obsession with technology has turned us against ourselves."

"Huh?" Chati made a face as though she had just smelled her brother's dirty gym socks.

Sally searched for a bit of Tone Death trivia that might impress. "Also, their lead guitarist uses a special kind of makeup to look like a corpse!"

Chati took two slow steps back before turning and walking quickly away. She never asked about one of Sally's T-shirts again.

"May I help you?" a nasal voice blared through the Vanderperfects' intercom.

Sally slipped from her post against the gate. Tucking her hair behind her ears, she cleared her throat. "Oh, um. I'm waiting for Viola, please. I'm Sally. Sally Simple—"

"Miss Vanderperfect will be out presently." The intercom clicked off, and Sally resumed biting her nails.

Viola Vanderperfect had been Sally's best friend when they were babies. They were born on the same day, and the girls' mothers met in the maternity ward when a nearsighted nurse accidentally switched the bassinets. Choosing laughter over lawsuit, the Vanderperfects and Simplesmiths became fast friends. For the two years that followed, their daughters were almost never apart.

When the Vanderperfects moved from the sleepy town of Merryland to seek their fortune in the hustle and bustle of Watta City, the families promised to visit often. But when Sally's mother became ill, that promise grew difficult to keep. By the time Mrs. Simplesmith died, eight years had passed without a single visit. Aside from the occasional birthday card and coupon books for their wildly successful chain of nursery-rhyme-themed restaurants, the Vanderperfects fell out of touch.

None of this was more than a distant memory to Sally until two weeks ago, when her father received a letter with a Watta City return address.

"Oh, hey, kiddo. I almost forgot to tell you," Mr. Simplesmith said as he rushed off to the research lab where he all but slept. "The Vanderperfects are moving back here at the end of the month. Remember your friend Viola? Looks like she'll be joining your class. See you around, Sal!"

Had Mr. Simplesmith not been so consumed with balancing his coffee cup on a stack of papers while acrobatically closing the door with his right elbow, he might have noticed his daughter frozen in place, the spoonful of cereal dripping milk as it approached her gaping mouth.

Within moments of regaining movement, Sally had written and mailed a letter to Viola reintroducing herself and offering to accompany her long-lost friend to her first day of school. A week later a reply arrived from Mrs. Vanderperfect with directions to their new home and an invitation to come early to join Viola on her morning dog walk.

Now that the reunion was finally here, Sally's boldness gave way to alarm. Would Viola indeed be the death-rock-loving kindred spirit of whom Sally had dreamed? A strong gust of expensive perfume snapped her back to the present, where a perfectly manicured woman with arms raised in a wide V came running down the estate's long drive.

"Sally, Sally, Sally!" Vivienne Vanderperfect burst through the gate and blew two air kisses at the wide-eyed child. "So, this is what you grew up to be." Mrs. Vanderperfect's smile faded slightly. "How…unique."

Sally bit her lip.

"I'm sorry, I just assumed you'd be more like your mother. The way that woman could command a room just by entering it." Vivienne gazed into the bright blue sky. "She was the toast of Merryland without making the slightest effort. She was such...an inspiration." Glancing back at Sally, she added, "Ah, but you do have her eyes."

Sally blushed. "Thank you, Mrs.—"

"Oh, now, darling, call me Vivienne. Viola's just grabbing Princess Poopsy Von Vanderpoodle's leash, and then I'll let you two be off!" Vivienne looked Sally over before ultimately nodding her head in approval. "Yes, I can tell my Vi will have a powerful effect on you, Sally. And you can be there for her. Just like I was for your mother."

Vivienne's eyes teared, and Sally pinched her own skin to stop from breaking down. Despite her obvious reservations about Sally's appearance, Mrs. Vanderperfect's determination to reach out to her dead friend's daughter suited Sally just fine. It was Viola she was here for, anyway; the friend she had waited for all her life.

One last time, Sally called up the picture of Viola she had been perfecting all week. In it, Viola wore a dog-collar necklace that complemented Sally's T-shirt of Tone Death's latest album: *You Can't Put Me in the Doghouse—I Already Live There*. In Sally's imagination, Viola already had three piercings in her left ear, including one up at the top, in the exact spot Sally's father refused to consider until his daughter turned eighteen. In her mind, Viola was everything Sally was not quite, but that she could surely become, with a little help from an old friend.

Of course, what Viola Vanderperfect turned out to be was something Sally was not at all. The real Viola gracefully glided to her mother's side. Her strawberry-blond hair bounced and swayed as though a hidden fan was blowing only on her. Her white sweater and pink skirt adorably complemented the white poodle in a pink sweater that heeled elegantly at her side. A bright smile of impossibly white teeth blossomed on Viola's face, and Sally could have sworn she saw an actual twinkle in the most perfect Vanderperfect's eye.

"Sally, it's been such a long time. Would you care to join Princess Poopsy and me on our walk?" Viola fluttered her eyelashes. Though she looked nothing like what Sally had pictured, she seemed friendly enough.

"Uh, yeah. OK. Sure."

Viola kissed her mother good-bye, and Sally followed the beautiful girl and her well-groomed dog onto the sidewalk. While they pranced, she lumbered. While they nimbly skirted trash cans and baby carriages, Sally tripped over a toddler, making him cry. Finally turning onto a quiet side street, Sally sighed with relief that they were alone.

The mismatched girls continued to walk in silence. On Sally's part, she simply did not know what to say to this girly girl. A poorly chosen opening had damaged potential friendships before, so Sally kept her mouth shut, hoping Viola would be brave enough to break the ice.

Sally was focused on Princess Poopsy's unparalleled

prance when Viola finally made a peep. "*Peep, peep!*" she said to Poopsy, who obediently squatted on the grass.

"Wow! That was amazing! How'd you do that?" Sally asked, her vocal paralysis forgotten.

"Impressive training and impeccable pedigree," Viola singsonged. Her airy voice lilted like a lullaby. It was so soothing that, at first, Sally didn't notice the dark scowl that had eclipsed her companion's face.

"Unlike Princess Poopsy, both training and pedigree are virtues that you, Sally Simplesmith, will never possess. After today's obligatory get-together, you will be worth no more of my time, and I needn't take up any more of yours. We will part ways a few blocks from school, after which we'll only ever have to pass each other silently in the halls. Are we clear?" Viola's raised eyebrows seemed to indicate that she awaited a reply.

"But we used to—" was all Sally managed before Viola interrupted with such an honest laugh that, had any passersby heard it, they'd have thought these girls were enjoying themselves immensely.

"Wait—wait," Viola blurted between fits of hysteria. "You actually thought someone like me would be friends with someone like you? But why? You're nothing special. You're not even fit to be friends with my dog!"

Sally's skin began to prickle, and her cheeks stung as though they had been slapped. Composing herself, Viola leaned in close. "Sally, sweetie, let me make this perfectly clear. If you tell anyone that we were childish enough to be friends when we were babies, your days as a lovable loser will be over."

Smiling brightly, the stunningly pretty and breathtakingly mean Viola Vanderperfect linked arms with the girl she had just crushed and guided her back to the estate's front gate.

"Wait here for me, won't you, Sally?" Viola asked, loud enough for her mother to hear. "I just need to grab my bag, and then we can go!"

Sally saw Vivienne Vanderperfect smile as she watched the girls from her kitchen window. She opened her mouth to say something—anything—that would expose Viola as the terrible fraud she was.

"Uhn…" was the only sound that came out.

Chapter 2

VIOLA KEPT HER PROMISE and ditched Sally a few blocks from school. “Stay out of my way or it'll be your funeral,” the nasty new girl threatened. By the time Sally had convinced herself that dropping out of the sixth grade was not an option, she was late for class.

“...Ronald, Susannah, Tommy, and Zeke!” Sally entered the classroom just as Viola completed roll call to thunderous applause. Viola ignored the tardy girl, who slipped quietly into the back.

At recess, Chati Chattercathy led a gaggle of girls in recounting for Viola their favorite parts of their first impression of her. “For me,” Chati giggled, “it was when you asked if it was Chati with one *i* or two that I knew we'd be best friends!”

Sally lost control of the ball she was bouncing, and it hit Chati in the head. “Oh my gosh, Chati, I'm so—” Sally never got to finish her apology, for the victim chucked the ball back without ever acknowledging from where it had come. Chati continued her fawning as though she hadn't been interrupted at all.

Though Sally didn't quite click with her classmates, she had never been entirely ignored by them either. Suddenly she was invisible, thanks to a certain strawberry-blond bully who seemed to feed off undivided attention. By the time afternoon assembly rolled around, Sally was so alarmed that she kept looking at her hands, checking to see if she had disappeared completely.

The students of Merryland Middle School shuffled into their assembly seats and began the ritual of attempting to stay awake for the next forty-five minutes. But Sally finally had something to be excited about. The vice principal always read aloud the names of students with upcoming birthdays, and everyone was expected to clap. Sally loved hearing the applause after her name. She pretended that somewhere in the bleachers at least one kid was happy she had been born. This was her birthday month. Sincere or not, the applause would be just the pick-me-up she needed.

"And on the twenty-fifth, Tommy Gunn will turn eleven," Vice Principal Sergeant droned. While the rest of the students doodled or napped, Sally's excitement kindled, knowing that her name was next. "This year, the twenty-ninth is a very special birthday. In fact, it's two, as a pair of sixth graders shares this date of birth. Please put your hands together for our newest student, Viola Vanderperfect, and..."

The screams and cheers for Viola drowned out Sally's name. Even the jaded eighth graders went wild. Viola had captured the imagination of every kid at Merryland Middle School, and her rapid rise had come at Sally's expense. Though she had always been an outcast, this was the first time Sally felt cast out. As she listened to the applause that was not hers, she realized her life was over.

Chapter 3

SALLY SHOVED OPEN THE gate to Hope Hill Cemetery. As she trudged up the path, it began to drizzle. She contemplated shielding herself with her backpack, but it was too heavy to lift over her head. She was spent. All she wanted was to be done with it.

The spitting mist turned to heavy drops of water. By the time Sally reached her destination, she was drenched.

Sally collapsed on her mother's grave and recalled the day she had revealed her most secret wish. Patty

Simplesmith lay in a hospital bed, hooked up to more machines than Sally cared to remember. Her pale skin had yellowed slightly, and her lips were cracked despite the thirteen tubes of Chapstick that Sally had given her; one for each day spent in this hospital room. "I want to come with you, Mom," Sally had said softly. She did not look her mother in the eye.

"You can't, baby. Not yet," Patty whispered. The beeps and clicks of the machines blared over her weakened voice.

"Then when? I don't belong here without you."

"Yes, you do." Her mother smiled.

Sally rolled her eyes. "No, I don't. I never have! They'll never be…They only see me when I'm with…" Sally turned away, not wanting her mother to see the tears she could not stop. Quietly, she added, "If you get to die, then I want to too."

"Sally!" Mrs. Simplesmith's voice was suddenly strong. The dying woman, barely able to lift a finger for the past two weeks, gripped her daughter's wrist. "Sally, promise me you'll give this life everything you've got."

"Mom…" Sally's eyes widened, surprised by the frail patient's sudden vigor. She placed her free hand over her mother's and squeezed it tightly.

"Promise me!" Patty searched her daughter's face in desperation.

Sally opened her mouth to assure her mother that she wouldn't do anything reckless, but when she spoke, her words were full of spite. "Sure, thing, Mom. After you're gone, I promise to try as hard as I can to be A-OK so long as you promise that when I fail spectacularly and it so totally doesn't work out, you'll be able to fix it."

Sally's voice grew louder, and she began to tremble. "Yeah," she continued. "In fact, Mom, promise me that, alive or dead, you'll always take care of me, that when I need you, you'll give me whatever I want to make things right, and I'll live every stupid day to the fullest. If you can promise me that, then we've got a deal."

Sally's chest heaved, and she looked away from her mother. When her breathing finally calmed, she blushed, embarrassed by her outburst. She had cleared her throat and prepared to apologize when Patty said, "Deal."

"What?" asked Sally.

"I said, we have a deal," Patty replied flatly. "Agreed?"

Sally had never known her mother to lie, and she doubted she would start on her deathbed. After a moment of stunned silence, Sally nodded. "OK, Mom. Agreed."

Loosening her grip on her daughter's wrist, Patty's voice grew quiet once more. She managed a weak smile. "Good. Now, why don't you go eat something, Sal? You've been here for hours. You must be hungry, and I need to rest."

"OK," Sally agreed. Fearful of upsetting her mother further, she turned to leave.

"Hey! Not so fast," Patty said. She craned her neck so that her nose stuck up in the air. Leaning down, Sally gently touched her own nose to her mother's. They wiggled them in unison, a special gesture just for them. "Love you, kid." Patty smiled. Sally kissed her on the cheek and headed to the cafeteria.

By the time she returned, her mother had died.

Though she cried at the funeral, Sally did not allow her tears to turn bitter. She was determined to keep the promise she had made to her mother, not least because it was the last thing they had ever discussed. Sally would give in to this life and do her best to find others with whom to live it. But after the initial public sympathies died down, she discovered she was more alone than ever. Viola Vanderperfect had been her last hope for the true friend her mother wanted for her. With that dream shattered, Sally decided that there was nothing for her in this life.

I want to come with you, Sally thought as she lay on her mother's grave. Though it was still raining, the oak tree above provided welcome shelter. Wiping her tearstained face, Sally shimmied her back against her mother's headstone and addressed the dead.

"I think it's time you lived up to your end of the bargain," she whispered. "I tried it your way. It didn't work, and today was a big old nail in that coffin…no offense." Thunder cracked, and Sally hugged herself tightly.

"The evidence is clear. The verdict is in. No one cares one bit about me, not like you did. Not half as much as you did." Sally nestled deeper into the wet earth. "I'm tired of waiting for someone, *anyone* alive and willing to bother with me. Now it's time to keep your promise. Give me what I want." She inhaled deeply, filling her lungs with resolve. "Give. Me. Death."

The wind, which had been frantically howling in the trees, suddenly calmed. The leaves on the branches stilled. For a moment, all sound and movement ceased, and Sally willfully gulped down the rising lump in her throat.

A flash of lightning streaked through the sky and hit the great oak above the grave. Sally saw a blinding white light before everything went black.

Chapter 4

SALLY FELT A LIGHT wind tickle the back of her neck. Facedown in the mud, she instinctively inhaled, and her nose and mouth filled with dirt. Her body jerked backward and she coughed up mounds of soil, frantically clawing muck away from her eyes. She alternated between ravenously sucking in air and violently gagging on it, until her breathing finally became even.

Sally focused on the landscape before her. The giant oak that towered over her mother's grave had split in two. The headstone was partially crushed by a fallen branch. All around her lay debris. And yet, by some unhappy miracle, Sally was intact. What had happened to her was not death at all. It was simply the continuation of hell on earth.

Sally crawled to the ruined headstone and traced her fingers over the letters that remained.

"Patricia Simple...Beloved Moth...Born 19...Died." Though it stung her throat to speak, Sally thought she might feel comforted by the sound of something other than the howling wind. She did not. Tears turned quickly to heaving sobs. Sally's body shook in spasms she thought would never cease. She flung herself onto the ruins of her mother's grave and closed her eyes.

She had been lying motionless for nearly ten minutes when something cool and smooth brushed against her cheek. She sat up with a start. Looking around frantically, she thought she saw a flash of white disappear behind a nearby headstone. She shut her eyes tight. What horrible thing had she called upon herself? Too afraid to move, she remained stock-still, hoping that if she saw no evil, there would be none to fear. But a few moments later, the chilly, hard thing ran across her other cheek. Sally let out a sharp scream and buried her head in her sweater.

"No more," she shouted. "I'm sorry I wished for something I shouldn't have. Just leave me alone, please. I've had enough!"

For a good long while there was only silence. Sally finally decided she was alone and whatever she had sensed was in her imagination. She nervously smoothed her hair and pushed it behind her ears. Cautiously, she opened her eyes. She saw nothing but the split oak and her mother's ruined grave before her.

Sally stood up, brushed as much dirt as she could from her damp clothes, and turned to head home. She managed only a single step before she saw the bright-smiling, tail-wagging skeleton dog beaming up at her.

Sally swooned, her knees buckled, and she collapsed in a faint.

The first time Sally regained consciousness, she screamed at the sight of the little dead dog, still panting and grinning by her side. She promptly passed out again. On her second reawakening, Sally stayed conscious long enough to scramble backward, putting some distance between herself and the petrified pooch. Imagining this to be a game, the animal bounded toward the frightened girl, his leathery tongue flapping and his bony tail wagging in delight. As he leapt onto her lap, Sally fainted once more.

The third time Sally came to, the dog had moved farther off and sat with his back to her. He turned his head to confirm that she was awake, then sighed dramatically before lying down in the opposite direction.

Now that the feisty, albeit filleted, Fido was pouting elsewhere, Sally began to process the dearly departed doggie's sudden appearance. "I guess when I asked for death I could have been more specific," she muttered to herself. The pup's remarkably well-preserved floppy ears perked up at the sound of the girl's voice. He turned to get a better look.

"H-hi, mister, uh, mister bone dog guy, I guess? I'm Sally. Sally Simplesmith."

The dog raised his snout and sniffed in her direction.

"So, uh, what were you? You know, before you died? You look kinda small." Sally heard a low growl. "Not in a bad way!" she quickly added. "I mean, you still look really strong with that big chest, or, um, exposed rib cage of yours." Sally whistled as the skeletal dog puffed out his chest, modeling his compact but sturdy physique.

"Wow," she marveled. "I bet your bark was a lot worse than your bite with that kind of lung capacity." The animal furrowed his brow and cocked his head to one side, dropping his pancake-shaped ears back. "I mean, when you had lungs, that is. I mean, not that you were all talk and no action either. I mean…what do I mean?"

Regarding Sally through huge, unblinking black eye sockets, the dog sighed and lay down again.

"So, you, uh, like this place?" she asked, changing the subject. "I think it's pretty nice, for a graveyard. My mom's buried here. Are you?" The dead dog yawned and rested his chin on the ground.

Sally absently chewed her fingernails. "Well, there's an

achievement. I've bored something to death that's already dead." Chuckling a little at her own joke, Sally realized that this was the first time she had smiled all day. Soon she was laughing a bit harder, and before long, she was in full-blown hysterics, clutching her stomach and rolling around on the ground.

The cadaverous canine could hold his grudge no longer. Pulsing with the need to play, he ran over to the giggling girl and pawed at her jiggling belly. Before she knew it he had climbed onto her chest and pinned her shoulders to the ground with his front paws.

Sally froze. For a seemingly endless moment, she and the perished pup regarded each other in silence. Then the little dog leaned forward and touched his nose to Sally's. He wiggled it lightly against hers.

Sally gasped. "My mom used to..." she whispered. Then a smile erupted on her face and she threw her arms around her new pet.

As the clouds cleared and the moon lit the night sky, Sally and her dead dog cuddled, wrestled, and ran all over the graveyard. She was having so much fun that she scarcely remembered how terribly the day had begun. For the first time in a long time, all felt right in the world. But when she came across a pile of littered fried chicken bones and threw one for her new friend to fetch, he turned up his nose and refused to look at her. Immediately she realized her mistake.

"Oh my gosh! I'm sooooo sorry," Sally offered. "You're right. It *is* in poor taste for a dog made of bones to chew on a real one. How about this, instead?" She held out a small stick, and the dead dog panted his approval.

Later, during a game of tag, Sally made a most important discovery. While fleeing from the spirited skeleton, she tripped over a small, flat grass marker and landed in an open grave. "Bones, no!" she cried. The dog skidded to a stop and sat obediently, six feet above.

"Good boy," she said as she pulled herself out of the grave with the help of some conveniently exposed tree roots. "So, I guess your name is Bones?"

"GGGgggrrrr-uff!" the deceased mutt barked.

"Well, Bones. It's very nice to meet you," Sally said as she held out her hand. Bones placed his paw in Sally's palm and they shook.

As she tickled her new companion's actual backbone, Sally caught sight of her watch. "Yikes! It's 7:30, already? I've got to get home." Her shoulders slumped. "I guess I have to leave now, Bones. I really wish I didn't, but..."

"GGGgggrrr-uff! GGGgggrrr-uff!" Bones trotted over to Sally's backpack, grabbed its strap in his mouth, and lugged it over to her. She bent down to take the bag.

"Thanks—"

"Grwoof," Bones said as he turned away and dragged the knapsack to the cemetery's exit. Wagging his tail, he waited for Sally to catch up.

"You're coming home with me?" she asked, barely able to contain the smile that threatened to overtake her face. "OK! But let's be careful not to let anyone else see you just yet."

The dog's tail froze mid-wag, and his flat, round ears drooped.

"Not that everybody won't love you once they get to know you, of course," Sally reassured. She leaned down and pressed her nose to his. "Bones, you're the most amazing thing I've ever seen. You're special, and for the first time in my life I think I might be special too. Let's just get home so I can introduce you to my dad first. Trust me. OK?"

Bones pushed his snout forward and wiggled it against hers. In a booming voice, he replied, "GGGgggrrr-uff," and wagged his tail happily once more.

As the new friends prepared to go home for the night, a nearby bush began to shake. Blinded by their happiness, neither Sally nor Bones took notice. Indeed, not once during their entire meet and greet did either of them have any awareness of the hooded figure that lurked in the shadows, studying the duo, listening to their every word.

As Sally and Bones said good-bye to her mother's grave, the figure decided to let them pass…for now. It was not yet the moment to strike.

The autumn moon shone brightly on the revived girl

and her reanimated pet as they walked from the safety of the graveyard into the unknown dangers of the night.

Chapter 5

Mr. Simplesmith's introduction to his daughter's new pet did not go according to plan. In part, this was because Sally had no idea how her brainy father and bloodless hound should meet. When she rushed into her house, late for dinner, she muttered something to Bones about hiding in the bushes before closing the door in his face.

As Mr. Simplesmith passed the peas, a harrowing howl caught the absentminded professor's attention. "What was that?" Sally's father asked.

"What was what?" Sally replied nervously. "I didn't hear anything."

The howling began again.

"Oh, you mean that *Ow-wooh-wooh-wooh* noise coming from the front yard?" she stalled. "Probably just a squirrel… being eaten…by a bear. I hear it all the time when you're at the lab. Speaking of which, how was work today? Any earth-shattering breakthroughs? Wow, this chicken looks really great, Dad. Eat up! Yum!" Sally tore at her drumstick, stuffing her mouth with a much-too-large bite.

"Oh, the lab," replied her father, no longer distracted. "Yes, we made a fascinating discovery today. Remember that fruit fly we named Lance?"

"Ow-wooh-wooh-wooh." The howling grew louder, coming now from outside the kitchen where the Simplesmiths dined.

"A bear?" Sally's father murmured as he reached for a pair of barbecue tongs. Holding the makeshift weapon high in the air, he turned the knob of the kitchen door. Sally tried to call out, but the mouthful of chicken betrayed her. She began to choke.

Abandoning the partially open door, Mr. Simplesmith ran to his daughter's aid. Though he was a brilliant man, Seymour Simplesmith lacked common sense and basic life-saving skills. Leaning over his little girl as she turned blue from lack of oxygen, he helplessly called out, "Somebody, please! Help!"

"GGGgggrrr-ufff!" A compact but speedy little dog-shaped skeleton burst through the still ajar kitchen door. The clever cadaver leapt into the air and landed hard on Sally's constricted chest. The chunk of chicken dislodged, and Sally gasped herself back to a normal pigmentation. As her father hugged her, Sally began to cry.

"You're OK, now, Sal," Mr. Simplesmith reassured. He held his daughter close and stroked her hair.

"Bones! Bones!" Sally wiggled an arm free from her

father's embrace and held it out for her puppy. As the little corpse snuggled into Sally, her father fell backward.

"What is...*that?*" Mr. Simplesmith pointed with a trembling hand.

"It's all right, Daddy." Sally smiled through her tears. "He's my dog, Bones. I love him and he loves me, and he's part of this family now. OK?"

In theory, Mr. Simplesmith took no issue with encountering mysteries of the unknown. As a man of science, his life's work revolved around uncovering the explanations for such phenomena. Indeed, it was this passionate focus that both made him appealing to his late wife and often caused him to walk into walls. However, coming face-to-face with a lifesaving, lifeless dog was something else altogether.

"How did it...? Where did you...?" Sally's father shook all over.

"I found him at the cemetery." She hesitated before adding, "I think he was a present from Mom."

Mr. Simplesmith's body tensed. "Sally, I told you not to go there. It isn't a place for a young girl to be. And your mother isn't even there. It's just where her body is. It's not her. She isn't..." Mr. Simplesmith trailed off, unable to finish his painful thought. His eyes scanned the room for some touchstone with which to tie himself to a reality he could control. He found it curled up in his daughter's lap. "But this, this thing, here...I don't know what it is, but it isn't staying. It isn't, isn't—"

"Isn't what?" Sally shouted. She suddenly felt hot, even though shivers ran through her body. "Isn't possible? Isn't real? Look at him. He's right here, and he just saved my life. He's mine, and I won't let you take him away from me just because you don't like where he came from or can't figure out why he exists. Or because he reminds you of Mom." Sally spat the last words, and her father shrank back.

Mr. Simplesmith could only stare at his furious child. His mouth hung open, but no words came. Since Patty's death, the surviving Simplesmiths had each retreated into their own quiet worlds. Because this was how Seymour preferred to mourn, it wasn't until this moment that he even considered his daughter might have wanted to grieve differently. When Sally finally calmed, he moved cautiously to sit by her side.

"Sally, I don't understand this. I don't know what this is, how it's possible..." Mr. Simplesmith looked from his daughter to the creature she protected in her lap. "What I do know is that, no matter how much I wish it weren't the case, your mother is gone."

"But I'm here," Sally said tiredly. "And so is Bones. Please don't take him away from me. Please, Dad. Don't." Upon hearing his name, the little skeleton dog looked up at his friend and gave her a kiss. Sally hugged him tightly.

As Mr. Simplesmith searched the scene for something he could understand, he discovered one simple truth. In the soulful brown eyes of his daughter and the twinkling black orbs of her pet, he detected love. Though he could not imagine living with a corpse, neither could he bear to cause Sally more pain. He agreed to let Bones remain on the conditions that he stay off the couch and be kept their family's secret. Sally did not immediately agree.

"But wh-hy?" she whined. "Bones is amazing. Everyone will love him!"

"Many people will fear him," her father replied. "This thing—"

"Dog," Sally corrected. "My dog, Bones."

Seymour smiled faintly. "All right. Your dog Bones is…unique. And many people are afraid of things they've never seen before, especially when those things appear to be skeletal animals returned from the dead." Seymour leaned in a bit closer now, his scientific curiosity getting the best of him. "It is fascinating, though. How does he function without a central nervous system or organs of any kind? Hmmm…"

Mr. Simplesmith paced the kitchen. He picked up a drumstick and tapped it lightly against his lips. Knowing she had lost her father to the turning wheels of his singularly

brilliant brain, Sally shifted Bones off her lap and returned to the table. It had been a long day, and she was actually quite hungry.

"The chicken really is good, Dad," she offered brightly. "I meant what I said before I choked on it. Have some."

Mr. Simplesmith regarded the uneaten drumstick in his hand and shook his head. "I think I've had enough to digest tonight," he sighed. "Perhaps Bones would like some of the scraps, though? Here you go, uh, boy." His hands shaking slightly, Sally's father tossed the chicken leg at the lifeless mutt. Bones shuffled backward and shot Sally a horrified look. He opened his mouth to protest, but before he had the chance, Sally was speaking.

"Oh, gee, Bones. Isn't that soooo nice of my father? Giving you something he made himself in the hopes that you'd like it and would feel welcome in your new home?" Sally looked to Bones with pleading eyes. She nodded her head encouragingly, praying that he would pretend to like the marrowbones of dead animals just this once.

At first, the dead dog merely glared at her, unblinking and unyielding. Sally was about to confess her dog's deep disdain for the bone her father had gifted when the cadaver conceded. Sighing heavily, Bones took the meaty bone by its tip, careful to touch it only with his front teeth. He carried it behind Sally's chair and growled low so that only she could hear.

Mr. Simplesmith grinned. "He obviously likes being with you, Sal." His smile faded. "Which is problematic." He took a chicken wing and began to nibble on it.

"Come on, Dad," Sally said, rolling her eyes. "Do you really think an angry mob is going to knock down our door when they find out about Bones?"

Just then a gust of wind blew open the kitchen door, and a loud crash came from the yard behind the Simplesmiths' house. Seymour rose to check out the commotion, but Sally beat him to it.

"Ha ha," she laughed nervously as she pulled the door to her. "Guess we forgot to close up. Good thing it's just a windy night and this has absolutely nothing to do with your concern for Bones's safety."

Her father frowned. "It's not Bones I'm worried about, Sal," he explained as he returned to his seat. "Your pet's exposure could put us all in danger. I'm sorry, but your safety is my top priority. The deal is this—Bones can stay here, but only in secret. And if I get one whiff of any trouble, he's got to go. Understood?"

The deal was not at all understandable to Sally. But as she prepared to argue the point, she noticed a crisp white envelope taped to the garbage bin outside the kitchen door. Written on it in messy scrawl was her name. Though it was chilly outside, her shivering had nothing to do with the wind. She stepped out of the kitchen and tore open the envelope. Inside was an equally messily written note, but despite its questionable appearance, its message was clear.

Roses are red
Violets are blue
Keep the monster secret
Or I'll get you two!

Sally's normally pale skin turned ghostly white. She looked into her yard and could have sworn she saw a shadowy figure slip back into the night.

Could her father actually be right? It seemed someone else already knew about Bones and had not accepted him with the love that Sally did. Suddenly, Sally faced a choice, and the answer could not have been clearer. Being special could wait. The only thing that mattered was keeping Bones safe. Stuffing the note into her pocket, she returned inside and bolted the door behind her.

"OK, Dad. We'll keep Bones between us."

Seymour gobbled some more chicken, proud of himself for having reached his daughter through good sense and rational discourse. He did not notice that though Sally had returned to the dinner table, she'd lost her appetite.

"How's this for a plan?" Seymour offered. "While you're home, Bones can have the run of the house so long as he doesn't chew anything up. All other times, he can stay in the basement, like when you're at school—"

"Grwoof!"

"No!" Bones and Sally said in unison.

"We can't be apart," Sally explained as her pet leapt onto her lap.

"Why on earth not?" Seymour demanded.

Though Sally was desperate to keep Bones close, especially now that she knew he was in danger, she was also sure she could never let her father know about the threatening note.

"I mean, you saw what he did when I left him outside of our house," she tried. "He'll find a way to follow me to school, and he'll bark and howl until I can come out. By then everyone will know about him, and you said yourself we had to keep him our secret."

Mr. Simplesmith considered his daughter's hypothesis.

"I suppose you might be right," he conceded. "But there are quite a few issues we'll have to work out if Bones is going to be always by your side."

"Right," Sally agreed. "Like what?"

"Problem one: getting to school undetected." Seymour pulled a map of Merryland from a drawer beneath the kitchen counter. "What if you take Maplewood Terrace to Oakdale Lane to Forrest Drive? That should provide enough tree and shrub coverage to hide Bones the whole way there, right?"

"I think so," Sally said. Sometimes it was very convenient to have a genius for a father.

"But what to do once you're in class? Or are you planning to hide him in your desk?" Mr. Simplesmith chuckled at his own joke.

"Oh, I know!" Sally exclaimed. "Outside my classroom, there's an old garbage shed that nobody goes near. They all think it's haunted—dorks. Anyway, there's a dirty window that looks into my class. I can see it from my desk. If I sneak in there early enough, I can set it up so that Bones can watch me all day!"

"GGGgggruff!" Bones said, wagging his tail.

"And at recess, I'll hang out with you in the shed!" Sally kissed him on the nose and knew she would always protect him, no matter the cost.

"Surely your classmates will notice if you're gone for too long, Sal," Mr. Simplesmith interrupted.

"No, Dad. They won't," Sally quietly replied. Her father regarded her curiously, then returned to his chicken. He did not argue the point.

That night, as Sally lay in bed with Bones curled at her feet, she thought about the coming day. Though the anonymous note frightened her, she prayed that if she followed the instructions and kept Bones a secret, everything would be all right. For despite the danger, this was the first time since she could remember that she was actually looking forward to waking up in the morning. Smiling, she closed her eyes. But in that split second just before sleep took her, she recalled the shadowy figure from her yard as it slipped into the chilly, black night.

Chapter 6

Bones's first day of school went remarkably according to plan. Mr. Simplesmith's assessment of the coverage the tree-lined route provided was exact. The abandoned shed proved a perfect haunt for Bones to haunt, and Sally's assumption that no one would miss her at recess was right on the money. Over the next few weeks, she continued to receive the occasional anonymous note, but they had become oddly encouraging, praising her secret-keeping skills and promising no harm would come to her or Bones if they kept up the good work. But still, the threat remained—keep the demon dog a secret or else! Sally had no intention of finding out what that meant.

Meanwhile, Viola Vanderperfect's *Operation: Pretend Sally Doesn't Exist* was in full swing, and Sally quickly turned this most painful indignity into her greatest asset. No one on the playground noticed when Sally ducked into the side alley at recess and didn't return until the end-of-period bell. None of her classmates seemed aware that she had stopped taking the bus to school in favor of walking an illogical and lengthy route. Nobody was the least bit concerned with anything having to do with Sally Simplesmith, and so they missed the fact that, for the first time in years, the usually gloomy girl was happy.

By the third week of Viola's reign, Sally found herself smiling all the time. She had even just about buried the icky feeling caused by merely thinking of her enemy. Sitting in the abandoned shed during recess one day, her skeleton dog cuddled into her lap, Sally marveled at how Viola's plan had backfired. "You know, I think Viola's evilness was actually a blessing."

Bones growled at the mention of his best friend's nemesis.

"Don't get me wrong," Sally clarified. "She's still the most vile, villainous, vomitrocious Viola in the universe. I'm just saying, if I have to find a silver lining in all this, it's you."

"GGGgggrrr-uff!" the canine corpse barked through the plush bone-shaped dog toy he held in his mouth. Sally had given him the toy to make up for her initial fetch faux pas, and it had quickly become Bones's most treasured possession. Smiling at her dearest companion, Sally gave the toy a playful tug.

"It's funny how easy it's been to live off the grid," she continued. "I mean, at recess, I just have to wait for Viola to do something exciting, like breathe, and everyone's attention turns to her." Sally regarded a dust bunny in the corner. "But it might be sort of fun to go a little more cloak-and-dagger with it all. You know, to have to be the slightest bit careful that someone might be watching me disappear into—"

The whistle signaling the end of recess blew. "OK, boy. You know the drill." Bones nimbly leapt from Sally's lap onto the window seat from which he could view her classroom. "Don't forget to keep an eye on me. I'll try to sneak in at least one funny face when I'm sure no one's looking. I think Zeke might've caught me yesterday when I touched my tongue to my nose and crossed my eyes. Good thing he already thinks I'm a freak." Sally laughed weakly.

Kissing Bones's head, she gave his toy bone a final tug before leaving.

Carefully making her way through the side alley that led to the schoolyard, Sally froze when she noticed a figure lurking in the shadows. To her stomach-churning surprise, it was Viola Vanderperfect.

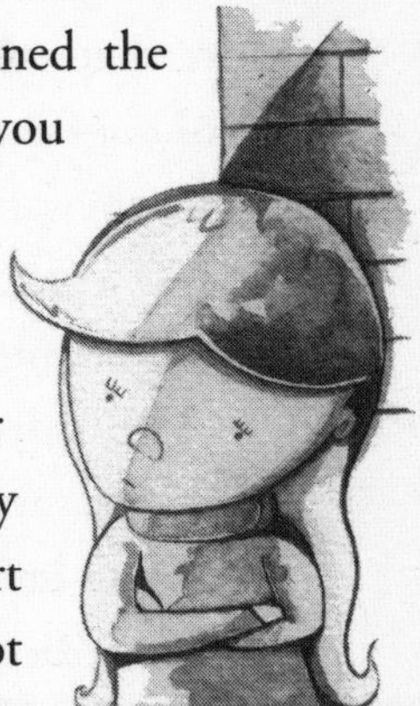

"Sally, we need to talk." Viola beckoned the startled girl, who reflexively obeyed. "As you know, my birthday is this weekend."

"Yeah," Sally timidly interjected. "It's my birthday too."

Viola frowned. "Duh! My mother wanted me to plan a joint birthday party with you. Can you believe it?" Sally's heart ached for the kindly mother that was not hers. "Obviously that was never going to happen," Viola cruelly snorted. "But I did have to promise her that I would invite you to my party."

Sally felt a small thrill at the prospect of attending what was sure to be the biggest social event of the school year. Despite herself, she smiled.

"Ew, no!" Viola snapped her fingers in Sally's face, bringing her back to reality. "Just because I have to invite you doesn't mean you'll be coming." Viola thrust a perfumed invitation into Sally's hand. "Call my mother and tell her you won't be able to make it. Tell her you're sick or something." Viola turned to leave but stopped dead in her tracks when she heard an unexpected voice.

"But I'm not sick," Sally said.

Viola spun around, a look of shock contorting her features into a horrible mask of disgust and terror. Though Sally had been keeping to herself out of fear of the anonymous note sender, something had changed in her over the past few weeks. She had gained a little bit of confidence, thanks to the unconditional love of a certain new friend. To both girls' surprise, Sally spoke the last words that either would have expected: "Maybe I'll, um, come."

Viola gasped and clutched her chest. She stopped breathing, and her complexion took on a blue tint. Squeezing her free hand into a fist, she began punching herself in the thigh. Sally was about to run for a teacher when Viola finally exhaled. After smoothing the pleats of her plaid skirt for a full thirty seconds, she recomposed herself and smiled.

"Sally, you're absolutely right. I apologize for being so rude. If you would like to come to my party, by all means, please do. After all, it is your birthday too." Viola put her arm around Sally's neck and led her from the shadows. "In fact, we really should celebrate your birth as well. How about this afternoon? We can invite everyone at school, including the teachers, and meet at, oh I don't know, the abandoned garbage shed?" Viola's eyes narrowed, and her grip on Sally's neck tightened. "You know the one. It's right outside our classroom. In fact, that's it right over there."

Sally's stomach plummeted, and she began to sway. Viola steadied her in a headlock. "You think I don't know about your creepy little loser hideaway?" the merciless mean girl whispered. "You've been going there every day at recess."

"No, I..."

"Relax." Viola released her grip, and Sally staggered to the wall. "I don't care what you do in there, so long as you're out of my sight. But it sure would be a shame if anyone else found out about it, don't you think?" Behind Viola's angelic smile Sally could have sworn she saw fangs. "Gee, Sally, you don't look so good. Are you sure you're feeling all right?"

Wearily, Sally regarded the cruelest creature on earth. "I...I think I am feeling a little sick."

"Good girl," Viola said as she patted Sally on the head. She turned and began to walk away. "Now, don't forget to contact my mother," she called over her shoulder. "She's having the whole thing catered in the estate's garden, so she'll want an accurate head count by tonight." Glancing back, she added, "Hope you feel better, Sally."

Viola returned to the noisy schoolyard, and Sally was once again alone in the alleyway. Running to a nearby garbage can, she managed to pull back her hair just as her nerves overtook her and she threw up.

Chapter 7

On the evening of the twenty-ninth, the Simplesmiths celebrated Sally's eleventh birthday. Though she requested dinner at home, her father insisted that they dine out. It had long been their tradition to celebrate big events at the local theme restaurant. It was owned by Vivienne Vanderperfect, who had sent Mr. Simplesmith enough coupons throughout the years to feed an entire village. Painfully aware that Viola would be enjoying her own party at home, Sally felt confident that this was the one time she would be safe from running into her nemesis at the Vanderperfects' establishment.

Sally's one birthday stipulation was that Bones be in attendance. "I wouldn't have anything to celebrate without him," she whined.

"I thought you might feel that way, Sal. So, I made you something." Mr. Simplesmith whistled, and Bones trotted into the living room, dragging a black vinyl bag with a bow on it.

Though he had not cut back his long hours at the lab since Bones's arrival, Sally's father had seemed a bit more present when at home. Instead of talking at Sally about his scientific studies, he more frequently asked about his daughter's day. He smiled at her tales of sneaking into the garbage shed and occasionally even laughed at her reenactments of Bones's adorable antics. It was not the relationship Sally had dreamed of, but it certainly was a start.

Sally's father unzipped the top flap of the bag and motioned for Bones to get in.

"It's a carrier. You wear it like a backpack," Mr. Simplesmith explained. "It has a tinted window panel that Bones can see out of, but people can't see in. I wasn't sure if he needed air, so I added some ventilation flaps just in case. It's a little bulky, I know, but I designed it with equal weight distribution in mind and for maximum comfort for a girl your size."

Tears filled Sally's eyes. Her father frowned and nervously pinched his thumbs. "Hey, Sal, if it's not what you want—"

Sally threw her arms around her father's neck. "This is the best present ever, Daddy."

Mr. Simplesmith hugged his daughter tight.

Despite the pouring rain, Miss Muffet's Morsels: Everyone's Favorite Theme Restaurant was packed. Even the private rooms that were normally opened up for busy rushes were booked. The longer the Simplesmiths waited, the more anxious Sally became that someone would discover what lurked inside her fancy new backpack.

When they finally settled into a booth at the back of the restaurant, Sally was too keyed up to even look at the menu.

"Can't decide between Peter Piper's Pickled Pike and the Baa-Baa-Blackened Sheep. What do you think, kiddo?" Mr. Simplesmith's eyes twinkled through his bottle-thick glasses. As stressed out as the situation made Sally, it seemed to have the opposite effect on her father. Seymour was giddy at the thrill of their covert operation. Twice, he even patted Bones's carrier in what seemed like genuine affection.

"They say the best seafood comes from chain restaurants," Sally offered.

"Then pike it is!" Her father waved for the waiter.

Though Sally had always considered the food bland and the waitstaff embarrassing in their nursery rhyme regalia, tonight at MMM's was different. Thanks to her father's excitement and her dog's presence, Sally gave in to the feeling that this dinner was indeed special. Soon, everything tasted, smelled, and felt better than ever before.

When it came time for dessert, Sally couldn't wait to hear "Happy Birthday" sung just for her. She didn't roll her eyes when two busboys dressed as Jack and Jill offered to fetch them pails of water. She didn't argue when Mr. Simplesmith handed her the plastic tiara he had forced her to wear at every birthday as long as she could remember. She even bounced a little when she detected the glow from a candle headed in her direction.

Grinning as Littles Boy Blue, Bo Peep, and Jack Horner sang "Happy Birthday" in imperfect harmony, Sally slipped her hand into Bones's carrier. She tapped his back to the rhythm of the celebratory song.

Sally and her father were enjoying their cake when the costumed waiters walked by singing "Happy Birthday" again. She turned to see the lucky patron with whom she shared this special day. The door to a private room swung open, and Sally spit out her food. Sitting on a bedazzled throne between Chati Chattercathy and Tommy Gunn was none other than Viola Vanderperfect, donning her own twinkling tiara and touching her cheek in fake surprise that all this trouble had been gone to for her.

"Dad, we have to go." Sally grabbed Bones's carrier and started for the exit.

"But, Sal, your Pat-a-Cake," her father protested. When Sally didn't stop, he helplessly added, "I haven't even paid the check yet."

Sally turned to respond and knocked into one of the Three Blind Mice, who was carrying a second cake to the private party room. Desperate to save the careening confection, the visually impaired rodent lunged and crashed into Peter Peter Pumpkin Eater, who in turn fell over Sally. Bones's carrier skidded across the dining room floor, and the top flap sprang open, releasing the cooped-up cadaver. The birthday cake flew through the air and landed on Sally's head.

Having heard the commotion, Chati Chattercathy was first on the scene. "Sally?" she asked, poised to get the scoop. "What are you—?" Before the gossipy girl could interrogate, something caught her attention that rendered her speechless for the first time in her life.

What appeared to be a dog made out of bones had jumped onto Sally Simplesmith's lap and was frantically licking her face. The creature grinned wildly and wagged its furless tail in delight.

The party guests surrounded Sally and her skeleton pup. No one said a word. When Bones had licked off all the frosting, he turned toward the crowd. They gasped in unison and clutched each other tightly, but no one ran.

For a long time there was only frozen silence. Finally, Bones caught sight of something intriguing and let out a low growl. Sally's eyes landed on Viola, who had moved to the front of the pack. In her arms was Princess Poopsy Von Vanderpoodle, oblivious to what was going on around her. The pampered pup was too busy chewing on a fuzzy toy bone.

Before Sally could stop him, Bones sprung at Viola, who shrieked and dropped the preoccupied poodle. The toy fell from Princess Poopsy's mouth, and Bones scooped it up.

Unlike the people who ran screaming from the dead dog's path, Princess Poopsy was in hot pursuit. She cared only about catching the little thief and engaged in a grand game of chase. Bones could not have been more thrilled.

"What *is* that thing?" Viola screamed at Sally, who was now on her feet. Her mind raced. This was it, everything her father had warned her about was happening, live and in Technicolor. Her only friend in the world had been exposed. Would he be taken from her? The loneliness she would endure would be nothing compared to the unbearable guilt she'd feel at having exposed him to the cruelty of mankind! Would scientists experiment on him in their search for a link between this world and the next? Would religious fanatics cite him as a sign of the coming apocalypse? Would they put him on display at a zoo or, worse yet, make him the spokespuppy for a trendy line of antiaging cosmetics?

Sally surveyed the room. Trembling, she prepared herself for a fight. But something was off. These were not the expressions that had haunted her dreams. The angry mob whose fear had turned to bloodlust was not here. Instead, her classmates and neighbors seemed more intrigued than incensed. At the far end of the dining hall was a group of girls standing on chairs and giggling hysterically every time Bones and Poopsy looped past. When Bones bounced off Miss Muffet's tuffet, they shrieked and clapped.

Nearby, Tommy Gunn cheered the dogs on, rallying the other sixth-grade boys in a chant of, "Go, Skeletor, go!" In a large booth, a family of five resumed eating, as though they were simply taking in some energetic dinner theater. And in the corner stood Sally's father, his hand loosely over his mouth, barely bothering to cover his wide smile.

Sally stood up tall. "That *thing* is my dog," she told Viola. "His name is Bones, and he happens to like Princess Poopsy's toy." Sally whistled, and Bones careened around a corner, skidding to a halt by her side.

"Drop it, Bones." The dog obeyed, and Sally picked up the toy. Princess Poopsy sidled up to her new playmate, whom she now found infinitely more interesting than anything else in the room. Sally handed the poodle the plush bone. Poopsy tossed it back at Bones, hoping for another chase.

"Poopsy, no," Viola commanded. Poopsy cowered slightly and tucked her tail between her legs.

"I thought I told you to stay away from my party," Viola whispered so only Sally could hear.

"I thought it was at your house," Sally replied in a normal voice.

"It was supposed to be in the garden, but it started to rain!" Viola hissed. "We moved it to *my* restaurant. Emphasis on *my!*"

"Last I checked, this was your mother's place," Sally snapped.

"Last I checked, I told you stay away from anything having to do with me," Viola spat. "Just look at you. You ruin everything. You really are a freak." Quietly she added, "Is that why your mother died? Couldn't stand the shame of having you for a daughter anymore?"

Sally flinched. The standoff was over. Viola had won. Sally stared at the ground.

"Come on Bones, let's go," she finally said, still unable to look anyone in the eye. Slinging the empty carrier over her shoulder, she headed toward the exit.

Bones regarded Viola and Princess Poopsy. With his paw, he shoved the toy bone at the unhappy poodle. Trotting after Sally, he stopped briefly at the door and turned to face his audience. "Grwoof!" he barked once before marching out.

That night, as Sally lay in bed pretending to be asleep, she wondered how things could get any worse. Just then, a chilly wind blew through her partially open bedroom window, and when she got up to close it she noticed a single white envelope taped to the sill. It had her name on it.

I warned you, the anonymous note read. *But you didn't listen. I'll get you, my pretty, and your little dog too!*

Sally shivered all over. What was she supposed to do? She looked at Bones, sleeping so peacefully on her bed, and suddenly, she knew. No matter the question, the answer was right there before her. She crumpled the note and threw it in the trash. Getting under the covers, she pulled her pup to her, cradling him in her arms. Though she was frightened of what tomorrow might bring, she now understood she could no longer hide from it. Sally Simplesmith didn't want a fight, but if that was what it had come to, she was ready for it.

Chapter 8

THE MONDAY AFTER BONES'S coming-out party, Sally decided to take the bus to school. Now that the dog was out of the bag, she no longer saw any reason to keep her friend under wraps. With her books clutched to her chest and Bones hanging out of the carrier on her back, Sally arrived at the bus stop.

Because it had been a while since she'd opted for automotive transportation, Sally had left her house extra early to be sure she wouldn't miss her ride. As she rested her Bones on an empty park bench, she watched the early morning parade of dog walkers and joggers pass her by.

"Check out that little guy," Sally said as she pointed to a moping English bulldog. Though his owner pulled the leash with all his might, the immovable beast refused to budge. "Poor pooch seems down in the dumps. Maybe Viola Vanderperfect ruined his birthday too."

"Grwoof," Bones said as he nuzzled his nose into Sally's arm. She hugged him to show she was all right.

"That dog seems off his game too," Sally said in reference to a frantic Jack Russell terrier that raced from twig to stick, in search of something he clearly could not find. A little girl chased after him, leash in hand, but Sally didn't think the kid stood a chance.

"Ggruff, ggruff!" Bones added, pointing his snout toward the jogging track that circled Merryland's reservoir.

"No way!" Sally gasped as she watched a pack of Pekingese pursue a terrified runner, yapping shrilly as they nipped at his heels. "What the heck is going on?"

"Something terrible, that's what," an approaching woman replied.

Sally recognized her neighbor and smiled. "Hi, Miss Punch," she said politely.

"Hi, Sally, honey," Judy Punch responded as she hurried past. "Sorry, darling. No time to chat. Mr. President and I are on a mission," the heavyset woman said, referring to the little dachshund that pulled her forward by his leash. "Pray for us that this horrible ordeal gets straightened out soon."

Before Sally had the chance to ask what she was talking about, Miss Punch and Mr. President were halfway down the block, and the school bus had arrived. Her concern for anyone other than herself and Bones instantly vanished.

"Here we go," she whispered to the creature in her carry-on as they boarded the bus.

The clamor of boisterous boys and gossiping girls died down immediately. Every eye was on Sally and the contents of her backpack. Dropping her head, she made for the nearest bench, managing to sit before anyone noticed how terribly her knees shook.

"Hey, Sally." Tommy Gunn and Danny Boi plopped onto the bench across the aisle from hers. Sally regarded them out of the corner of her eye.

"Yeah, so, crazy party on Saturday, huh?" Tommy continued. He looked at the little skull that peeked out of her bag.

"Wouldn't know. I wasn't invited," Sally said, staring ahead.

"Well, yeah. I mean, at the restaurant, then," Tommy stumbled.

"Yeah, at the restaurant," echoed Danny.

"You know, when your dog thing, or whatever, ran around and knocked into people and stuff?" Tommy shook his head at the memory. Sally tensed and placed a protective hand on Bones. "That was pretty, well, you know...cool."

"Yeah, cool," Danny agreed.

Sally whipped around to face the boys, who instinctively recoiled. "Cool?" She repeated the word as if Tommy had said it in Finnish.

"Heck, yeah," Tommy hollered and pumped his fist in the air. "Super cool! Skeletor there—"

"Bones," Sally corrected. "His name is Bones."

"Sure, OK." Tommy waved his hands in surrender. "*Bones* is a pretty awesome little guy. Maybe we could, you know, if you both wanted to, maybe check out the tire swing at recess?"

Sally's eyes bulged. She stared at Tommy until he began to shift nervously in his seat. She wondered if he had any idea to whom he was speaking. Sally had known Tommy since they were toddlers, but he had never so much as glanced in her direction. Could he actually be interested in befriending her now? As Sally opened her mouth to speak, a voice that was not hers replied.

"She doesn't want to play on some dirty swing set. Do you, Sally?" Chati Chattercathy asked. She shook her head vigorously, silently answering her own question, and Sally, hypnotized, mimicked the side-to-side motion. "You can spend recess with me and the girls." Chati pointed to a quartet of smiling, lip-glossed faces a few rows back. They waved in unison.

"Oh, well, I don't—"

"Of course, your dead dog can come too," Chati added emphatically as she slid onto the bench behind Sally's. Bones popped out of his carrier to greet her. Surprised by the sudden proximity to the object of her frightened fascination, Chati lurched back, breaking the spell she had cast over Sally.

"You don't have to be scared of him," Sally snapped, her face flushing red in knee-jerk fury. "He's not going to hurt you."

"I-I'm not," Chati stuttered. "I was just..." Tommy and Danny laughed, and Chati's lip began to tremble.

Though Sally's heart would not yet believe it, her head was beginning to make sense of what was happening. Bones was an overnight fascination, and, simply by association, Sally had moved up the sixth-grade social ladder. Still, despite the fact that, for once, the taunting wasn't aimed at her, Sally couldn't help but feel surprising, if somewhat irritating, pity for her embarrassed classmate. She glared at the laughing boys across the aisle. They immediately quieted.

"Never mind, Chati. It's fine," Sally sighed. "I was a little scared of Bones at first too."

"You were?" Chati asked breathlessly.

"Sure," Sally admitted. "But then I got to know him, and we've been best friends since." She tickled her little pet, who licked her in gratitude.

"Omigosh, you have to eat lunch with us, Sally," Chati declared. "I want to hear ev-er-ee-thing!" Chati shifted her gaze to the friendly corpse that panted happily at her. She leaned in a brave two inches and added, "Maybe, if I get to know Bones, I can pet him too?"

Sally shrugged and nodded. Clapping wildly, Chati returned to the back of the bus where her girlfriends waited for what was sure to be an exhaustively detailed debriefing.

Tommy and Danny continued to steal glances at Bones for the rest of the ride to school. Sally managed to ignore them until Bones, tired of the boys' obvious gawking, unleashed a tirade of fed-up barking, causing them to fall off their bench and into the aisle. Sally couldn't help but laugh.

When they arrived at school, Tommy called to Sally as they disembarked from the bus. "I know you're doing lunch with Chati today, but maybe we can hang tomorrow?"

Sally shifted from one foot to the other. "Um, maybe," she replied.

"Cool!" Tommy said. He and Danny high-fived.

Glancing over her shoulder at Bones, Sally shrugged. "Guess we're not in Kansas anymore, Toto."

"Grwoof," Bones agreed before slipping down into his carrier and out of sight.

As the students of Merryland Middle School shuffled through the front gates, few of them noticed the local lawman standing off to the side, surveying the crowd. Had they offered him a glance, as Sally did, they surely would have been drawn to the little man who skulked beside him. Squat and fat in a starched white uniform, he had a deeply creased scowl tattooed across his face and the words "Dog Catcher" embroidered on the breast pocket of his jacket.

Sally felt her breakfast like a brick in her stomach. She quickly looked away. "Stay cool, boy," she whispered to Bones. Camouflaging herself in a flock of fifth graders, she was nearly in the building when a familiar voice called out.

"Hey, Sally," said Officer Stu as he motioned her over.

His smile was wide, but his eyes looked troubled as they moved between Sally and her backpack.

"Hi, Officer Stu," Sally said in the calmest voice she could muster. "What's up?" She smiled at the lanky policeman, whom she had known since she was born. When her parents were given the wrong baby, it was Stu who solved the mystery of the mix-up. After that, he had always made time for Sally, and he was one of the few, if not the only, Merrylanders who seemed unfazed by her preference for graveyards over malls.

"Heard about your birthday dinner at Miss Muffet's," the kindly cop began. "Sounds like it was a real to-do." He paused, extending an invitation for Sally to take up the narrative. With her silence, she declined. "Well," he continued, "heard you had a special friend at that party. A different kind of friend. Want to tell me about that?"

Sally remained silent. She liked Officer Stu and might have told him everything were it not for the nasty troll-man loitering nearby, who licked his lips as he noisily sucked air in through his mouth. His squinty black eyes feasted on Sally's backpack, and she turned slightly, attempting to shield it from the grotesque gentleman's hungry stare. The bell signaling first period rang. Sally jumped.

"Whassa matter, girly?" asked the Dog Catcher. "You look a bit pale." The weaselly little man sucked on his teeth.

"Well, hah, if I hurry on to math, maybe sine and cosine could get me a good tan." Sally laughed feebly as beads of sweat erupted on her forehead.

"It's OK, Sally," said Officer Stu. "I'll make sure your teacher knows why you're late."

"He already knows why," the D.C. interjected. "It's because 'a what's in that bag. Let's rip it open and see what spills out." The little man lunged at Sally, who swerved out of his path.

"Now hang on a second," Officer Stu began, but it was too late. The D.C. had managed to grab hold of one of the ventilation panels on Bones's carrier. When Sally turned, he yanked, and the bag tore open. A bundle of bones tumbled out. Dazed from the fall, the skeleton puppy took a moment to locate his owner, but it was all the pint-sized bounty hunter needed to execute his attack.

A metal collar snapped around Bones's neck. It was connected to a long rod that the D.C. gripped triumphantly in his meaty little hands.

"Let him go!" Sally screamed. Bones barked and tried unsuccessfully to reach his distraught friend.

"Now, there's no need to get hysterical," Officer Stu lamely comforted, though he seemed as surprised as Sally by this turn of events. Turning to the D.C., he added, "And there's no need to lock the dog up. We agreed only to investigate the situation."

"What else is there to investigate?" the D.C. snapped. "A crime's been committed, and this *thing*'s the clear culprit!"

"A crime? What crime?" Sally demanded. "Bones hasn't done anything wrong!"

The D.C. snorted. "Oh, really? Then you tell me who's been stealing all the neighborhood dogs' bones?"

Confused, Sally turned to Officer Stu. "What is he talking about?"

The D.C. spoke before Stu had the chance. "Between 9:00 p.m. Friday evening—just after your little friend here made his demonic debut—and 6:00 a.m. today, nearly every bone belonging to a canine citizen of Merryland, USA, has been stolen. It's up to me to sniff out the guilty party."

The D.C. planted his feet firmly on the ground and put his free hand on his hip. Sally imagined him practicing this tough-guy stance in front of his mirror at home. Had he not had a vise grip on her pet, she might even have laughed.

"But that's crazy," she said as calmly as she could. "Why would anyone take dog toys?"

"I'm not talkin' fuzzy cloth playthings," the D.C. declared. "I don't even mean rawhides. Someone's been snatching bones. Real, marrow-filled bones! Just like the ones your pooch here is made out of." Leaning in close to the incarcerated cadaver, the D.C. bared his teeth in a triumphant grimace. "You're mine now, bub. I don't know what you are, but I intend to find out. I'm gonna give you a full examination."

Tears stung Sally's eyes as Bones tried in vain to free himself. Whistling lightly, the evil D.C. dragged his catch toward an imposing white van. Sally lunged forward, throwing herself on top of her pet.

"No!" she shouted as she pulled on his collar. "You have no evidence. You have to let him go."

"Evidence?" the D.C. scoffed. "He's a mange-less mutt! I'm taking him in."

Sally turned to Officer Stu, her onetime champion, tears streaming down her cheeks. "Do something," she pleaded. "Please!"

The lawman, who had been paralyzed for much of the scene, silently strode over to the D.C. and yanked the snare pole from his hands. "Let the dog go," he commanded.

"What?" the D.C. cried.

"Sally's right," said Officer Stu, keeping his cool. "You don't have any real proof that Bones here committed this crime. Everything you've said so far is purely circumstantial. Therefore, you have to set him free."

"But the town is going nuts!" the D.C. cried. "Dogs are rebelling everywhere—running wild at the dog park, going on hunger strikes in their homes—and their owners are calling for me. I'm the one who can help them." Pulling Stu aside, he added in a low tone, "It's my turn to be the hero. Don't take this away from me."

Stu pulled his arm from the little man's desperate grip. "Get me some hard evidence and we'll talk. Until then, there's nothing left to discuss."

The D.C. may have been a cruel gnome of a man, but he wasn't stupid enough to push Stu any farther. Instead, he scrambled for another way to keep Bones in his custody. "Well, what about his tags? The dog needs to be registered. I bet he doesn't even have a license!"

"I—I just got him...for my birthday," Sally improvised. "I was going to make everything official after school."

The D.C. snapped, "In Merryland, every dog must have issued a proper license within five weeks of birth. This mutt looks a heckuvalot older than five weeks. Without the proper papers, this pooch is impounded."

Without thinking, Sally said the first words that popped into her head. "Which birth?" she blurted.

"What?" the D.C. growled.

"Which birth?" Sally repeated, more confident now. The D.C. shook his head, still a few steps behind.

"Well, sure," Officer Stu chimed in. "That is, it seems to me this little fella's just had a rebirth of sorts. Now, Sally. Your dog wasn't a birthday present, was he?"

"No, sir," she answered.

"Where did you find him?" Stu asked.

Sally hesitated.

"The truth, Sally. Tell me where he came from."

"The graveyard. Where my mother's buried."

Officer Stu smiled. "Now, how long ago was it that he, uh, came to you?"

"Four weeks, sir," she said. "It's only been four weeks."

"GGGgggrrrr-uff!" Bones barked as he wiggled in his chains.

"And before that, you'd never seen him? In the graveyard or anywhere else?"

"No, sir!"

"Then I'd say the first recorded sighting is his official rebirth date." Officer Stu winked at Sally.

"Rebirth?!" the D.C. howled.

"Yes," Stu replied. "Rebirth. You think if this little guy was around before Sally found him, we wouldn't have heard? Practically the entire town knows about him after just one appearance on Saturday night. Now, I'm not saying I understand what he is or where he came from, but one thing I'm pretty sure of, this dog belongs to her." Officer Stu pointed at Sally and smiled. "You've got one week to get him a license."

"Yes, sir!" she agreed and turned to Bones's furious captor. "Can I have my dog back, please?"

"But—" he protested.

"Now," Officer Stu commanded.

With the dead dog once again in her arms, Sally

thanked the clever cop and promised to apply for Bones's license that very afternoon. But as she turned to enter the school, the D.C. cried out, "Living or dead, that animal cannot be allowed in the building! It would violate the sanitation laws of our county. Or are you planning to loosely interpret those too, Officer Stu?"

Ignoring the offense, Stu replied, "I suppose that no dog, no matter its flesh and blood status, should go into the school."

"But Bones isn't—"

"I think it'll be just fine for him to wait outside on the playground, though. That way, you can see him at recess, and he won't be wandering around town *unlicensed.*" Stu emphasized his final word. The D.C. snarled but said nothing. "I'll just let Principal Friend know about our arrangement. Now, why don't you take Bones around back and then get on into class. All right, Sally?"

"Yes, Officer Stu. I will," she replied. Before running off, she gave the policeman a brief, tight hug. As she and Bones hurried to the playground, Sally felt the D.C.'s fiery stare burn into her. Though she tried to convince herself otherwise, she knew this was not the last they'd heard of him or of the curious case of the bone snatcher.

Chapter 9

"AND HE WAS JUST there? Wagging and smiling and totally all yours?" Chati poked at Sally with a lightly nibbled celery stick. "That is like the most bestest present ever!" To no one's surprise more than her own, Sally Simplesmith sat at a picnic table in the schoolyard, her dead dog in her lap, surrounded by a pride of pretty-in-pink zombies who, until recently, could have cared less whether she lived or died.

"Yeah," Susannah Oh agreed. "I mean, my mother would never even consider a gift that wasn't from Trendy Wendy's. But your mom went out of her way to get the most specialest thing ever that is totally you…and she's dead!"

All the girls at Sally's lunch table nodded like bobble-headed dolls. All save one, whose blank expression and vacant eyes contrasted with her bouncy strawberry blond hair and perfectly rosy complexion. Indeed, Viola Vanderperfect seemed not to have moved an inch since Sally had accepted Chati's invitation to join them for lunch. She just stared beyond where Sally and

Bones sat, refusing to acknowledge them or react to this shameful charade.

"My birthday's coming up, and my parents want to take me and my friends to some sold-out concert," Chati sighed. "I mean, the tickets are basically impossible to get, but my dad owns the venue, so it's not like it's such a stretch. If they really understood me, like Sally's dead mother, they'd think of something so much better to get me."

"But you love music, Chati," said Susannah.

"Do, I? Or is music what my parents love, and am I just their puppet?" Chati bit off a chunk of celery and dropped her head on the table. Sally discreetly rolled her eyes at Bones, who pawed at his nose, attempting to cover his widening grin.

"I think it's nice of your parents to take you to a concert," Sally said in her most sympathetic voice.

"You do?" Chati asked, looking up.

"Um, sure. I love music. Well, most music anyway. And I've never even been to a concert. I buy all these concert T-shirts over the Internet just to feel like I was there. Your folks sound pretty cool to me."

"They do, don't they?" Chati agreed, satisfied. "Gosh, Sally, you are really deep."

As Chati and her friends considered the vast depths of Sally's mind, Tommy Gunn walked by the girls' table, hands in his pockets, eyes focused firmly on the ground. The extreme casualness of his stride seemed suspicious to

Sally, so she shouldn't have been so surprised when he suddenly bent down to re-tie his shoe right beside her.

"Oh, hey Sally," Tommy said, looking up from his already double-knotted laces. "Didn't see you there."

"Hiiii, Tommy," Chati cooed and poked Sally lightly in the ribs. Sally looked at Chati, not understanding, while the other girls giggled.

"So, uh, how's your first day with Skel—I mean, Bones going?" Tommy asked.

"Fine," Sally replied cautiously. Having so few friendly acquaintances had done nothing to help her skills at chitchat.

"Cool, good. That's, well, yeah, great." Tommy looked at his other perfectly tied shoelace and decided not to pretend it also needed to be tightened. Instead, he leaned on the table beside Sally and Bones and looked casually around the playground.

Although Sally was naïve, she was not dumb. She had seen these types of strange conversations before: though they had nothing to say, one or both participants wanted desperately to keep their interaction going and so talked about nothing much at all. Realizing that she was now on the receiving end of such an interaction, Sally suddenly felt confused, embarrassed, and more than a little annoyed. Was this a joke someone had put Tommy up to?

Over by the tire swings she saw Danny and some other boys looking in their direction. They were focused not just on Tommy, but on Sally too. Beside Sally sat Chati and her followers, staring at Tommy all gooey-eyed, hanging on his every word. But what convinced Sally that this had to be a trick was Viola. Though she still had not looked at Sally and seemed intent on ignoring the scene, Sally noticed that a little smirk had grown on her face. It was the only clue she needed. Her face flushed bright red at the exact moment that poor Tommy Gunn made a huge mistake.

"Oh, hey, so, like, what was up with that creepy guy with Officer Stu who was waiting for you outside school?" Tommy asked. "He looked pretty mad. Seemed like he was really after Bones."

Sally clutched the table. She thought there had been no witness to her terrible ordeal—one that she feared was far from over. So when Tommy jokingly added, "What'd Skeletor do to get on that guy's bad side, anyway? Break the law or something?" Sally snapped.

"I told you," she said angrily, rising to her feet. "His name is Bones!"

Tommy took a step back, utterly shocked. "I-I'm sorry," he stumbled. "I know his name, I was only saying…You know I just wanted…I didn't mean to…"

"Didn't mean to what, Tommy?" Chati demanded, standing now as well, showing Tommy that she had Sally's back. "Insult Bones again? Get his name right or get lost!"

Susannah and the other girls followed Chati's lead and

expressed their outrage to their poor confused classmate. It wasn't long before Tommy went on the defensive.

"Fine, whatever!" he cried. "I don't care about you or your creepy dog. I hope you both get whatever's coming to you. I was only talking."

Though Sally was unpracticed in the ways of middle school sparring, she had witnessed enough recess rows to know that this was her chance to silence her opponent with a particularly cutting remark. "Oh yeah?" she asked, sounding tougher than she felt. "Well, why don't you go talk somewhere else!"

Though it wasn't the most exciting comeback, Sally's sudden celebrity, mingled with the mood of the moment, allowed it to land like a Scud missile. The girls cheered as Tommy threw his hands in the air and stormed off.

Sally sneaked a peek at Viola out of the corner of her eye and saw that she was pouting again. Though she warned herself not to make a habit of this kind of talk, Sally had to admit that victory felt good.

As the excitement of the exchange died down, Sally became more and more embarrassed by her temper. Though her lunch mates seemed eager to discuss the interaction ad nauseum, Sally found herself wanting to talk about anything else at all. Unfortunately, Susannah changed the subject for her.

"So what was Tommy talking about?" she asked. "What did Officer Stu want with you?"

Sally flushed. "Oh, it was nothing," she replied. "Just something about some stolen dog stuff."

"Wait, I know about this," Chati chimed in. Sally wondered if there was anything Chati wasn't aware of. "So, my cousin, Vani, heard from our granny, Nanny, who heard from her neighbor, Tom, who heard from his mother, Mrs. Foolery, who heard from her gardener, Greenly Thum, who heard from his best friend, Officer Stu, that someone has been stealing all the neighborhood dogs' bones!"

"So?" Viola finally spoke. "Who cares?"

"A lot of people, from the sound of it," Chati continued. "Between the pound and the sheriff's office, the phone has been ringing off the hook with complaints. My puggle, Peaches, was entirely unimpressed by the vintage disco outfit I dressed her in this morning. It was tragic!" She turned to Sally. "What did Officer Stu talk to you about?"

Sally's mind raced. The last thing she wanted was for anyone to know that Bones was a suspect, especially now that she and Bones were just starting to fit in. "Oh, uh, he wanted to know if Bones had had anything stolen," she lied.

"Has he?" Chati asked, concerned.

"Nope. Last I checked, he's got all his bones right here," Sally joked.

"GGGgggrrrr-uff!" Bones barked as he leapt from his carrier and onto Sally's lap. The girls giggled and clapped.

"Anyway, Chati," Sally began, quickly switching topics. "The concert your parents are taking you to for your birthday—who's the band, anyway?"

"Well, that's the other problem," Chati sighed. "The band isn't one I've really head of. You know, it's so much less fun to dance onstage when you don't know what you're grooving to." The girls mumbled their agreement.

"Hey, wait a second," Chati suddenly remembered. "I think you know them, Sally. In fact I'm sure you've mentioned them before. The band's called something like… Stone Deaf?"

"Tone Death?!" Sally slammed her fists on the table and lurched toward Chati. Bones began to bark excitedly, and the girls shrunk back.

"Y-yeah, that's it," Chati stammered.

Recklessly abandoning her cool Q, Sally could hardly cover her disgust. Worse than making a fool of herself yelling at Tommy was knowing that tickets to see her favorite band would be wasted on Chati Chattercathy and her lamebrained friends. It was almost too much to bear.

"Wow." Sally's speech became robotic. "You are very lucky, Chati. Tone Death is my favorite band. Please let me know how the concert is." Closing her hands in tight fists, Sally dug her nails into her palms. To her surprise, Chati lit up like a firefly.

"Omigosh Sally!" Chati squeaked. "I just had the bestest idea. Why don't you and Bones come with us?"

"What?" Sally and Viola said in unison.

"Sure! I mean, I can't stand my cousin Vani anyway, so I'll just disinvite her and bring you instead. Ooooohhhhh, it'll be sooo cool to go to a death-rock concert with something that's really dead." Chati's minions clapped and cooed in agreement. For the first time, Viola looked at Sally with fury in her eyes.

It was bad enough that she had sat at Viola's lunch table, but Sally knew that to attend the same social function could only be seen as a direct challenge. Still, this was Tone Death. Sally could think of nothing, not even a majorly mad mean girl with a vendetta just for her, that could keep her away. She dared herself to say yes.

"Thanks, Chati," Sally said. "Bones and I would love to go."

"GGGgggrrr-uff!" Bones concurred, and the girls began to plan how to dress for the occasion. All except for Viola, who quietly rose from the table and exited the yard. No one but Sally noticed.

Chapter 10

"WE...ARE...TONE DEATH!"

Sally cheered along with hundreds of other Tone Death fans at the fully packed Chatter Hall. Bones howled happily in his carrier, and Chati, Susannah, and the other girls did their best to head-bang without messing up their hair. Only Viola remained in her seat, arms crossed and silent.

In the past few weeks, Sally's life had changed quite a bit. At lunch, she no longer sat alone; in gym class, she moved from last pick to first; on the bus, someone was always sure to save her a seat. The former social leper and her imperishable pet were overnight sensations. Even the anonymous notes had slowed down, and when they did arrive, they merely hinted at a day of reckoning Sally was starting to believe would never come.

Though she occasionally wondered whether or not her new friends were true, her desire to believe outweighed her fear. Even Bones's implication in the marrowbone thefts was concerning her less and less. Soon enough, Sally was having the time of her life.

"You were totally right!" Chati shouted in Sally's ear as the band played their number one hit, "Hearing Impaled." "Tone Death is the most awesomest death rock band ever! And the lead singer is a super hottie."

Sally laughed. "Frank Winston? I'm more of a Stein Whatley girl, myself." She blushed as she pointed to the shirtless guitarist, whose pasty skin glowed hauntingly under the blue-gel lights.

"Omigosh, that's perfect!" Chati screamed. "I'll take Frank, and you can have Stein."

"Yeah, in my dreams," said Sally.

"No, I mean now. When they take us up onstage, I get Frank, and Stein is all yours."

Before Sally could process what was happening, two large security guards had lifted her and Chati onto the stage. Chati, who had clearly done this before, ran over to Tone Death's lead singer and giddily giggled as he serenaded her. Sally, on the other hand, stood stock still, frozen in a spotlight while the guitarist glared angrily offstage at his manager.

She looked to the audience for help. Susannah shouted something and motioned for her to move right. The other girls displayed an array of uncomfortable expressions, from cringe-worthy grimace to embarrassed laughter. Viola, meanwhile, had finally found something worth getting to her feet for. Staring Sally down, she smiled triumphantly.

"Hey, kid," said a voice beside the frozen fan. "Don't think about the crowd. Just look at me."

Slowly, Sally turned to face the kindly stranger, but when she looked into Stein Whatley's graveyard-gray eyes, she felt her knees knock, her body sway, and her vision go a bit blurry. Instantly, she was short of breath.

Had this been the old Sally, she surely would have passed out right there, her moment wasted. But this Sally had a trick up her sleeve, an ace in the hole, a skeleton in her closet.

"GGGgggrrrr-uff!" Bones popped up from his carrier and planted his front paws on Sally's shoulder. He smiled brightly at the guitarist, who gasped in shock. Stein Whatley stumbled backward and would have fallen into the crowd had it not been for a dainty, pale hand that instinctively reached out to stop him. Pulling him toward her, Sally steadied the rocker, who stared at her in stunned silence. By now, the rest of his band had stopped playing and were looking at Sally and Bones, center stage, caught in a follow spot. Someone from the audience screamed, "What is that?" and Sally searched for the nearest exit.

She wondered how she could have been so stupid. Of course it had been too good to be true. The girls she had so desperately wanted to call friends must have set her up. Had they been waiting for the right moment to embarrass her all along? Sally tightened the straps of Bones's carrier and prepared to bolt. But before she had the chance, Bones leapt down onto the stage, spun once around the spotlight, and collapsed on his back. Stretching his legs high in the air, he rolled his head to one side. His limp tongue spilled out of his motionless mouth.

"Seriously, Bones?" Sally whispered. "You think *this* is an appropriate time to play dead?"

With nowhere to run, Sally moved farther into the spotlight. She reached out to Bones, prepared to protect him to the bitter end. But it wasn't the smooth skeleton of her pet that she suddenly felt against her skin. It was soft, human flesh. Stein Whatley had grabbed her hand in his. He raised it high.

"That," he shouted, "is rock and roll!" The audience erupted. Stein went on. "This next song's for the little lady who knows how to bring some afterlife to the party!" Chati ran to Sally and hugged her as the band began her favorite song, "Resurrection Complexion." Bones jumped to his feet, and the trio danced around the stage to the wild cheers of the crowd.

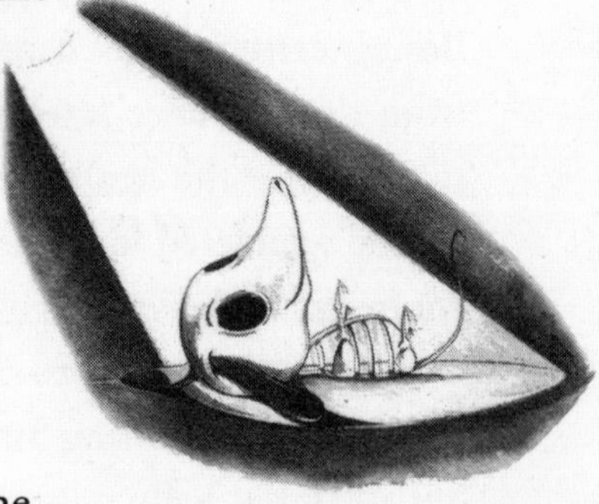

"Her skin's corpse white/ She's out of sight/She's calling me into the light," Frank Winston warbled into the mic. He held his hand out to Sally, who boldly took it. As he twirled her around the stage, Bones barked and chased his own tail in a never-ending circle.

"Got the kiss of death..." Frank let go, and Sally giggled her way back to Chati. She watched Stein play his guitar. She was losing herself in his amazing fingering when Bones's bark snapped her out of her trance. Tone Death's guitarist was moving toward her, his lead singer close behind.

"...She's out of breath..." Frank Winston held the mic to Sally's lips, cueing her to finish the lyric she knew by heart. Her mouth went dry; her lips felt chapped; her tongue stuck to the roof of her mouth. Sally looked to the audience. There were more faces than she could ever count, but only one stood out. Though her arms were still crossed and her features were frozen in a scowl, Sally could have sworn she saw Viola nodding her head along to the beat.

In a quiet but confident voice, Sally sang, "...She hits the spot like Miss Macbeth!"

The audience roared. Chati squeezed Sally tight. Stein Whatley winked at her as he took her hand and held it up again. Bones stood on his hind legs and barked, and Sally's porcelain-white skin turned a rarely seen shade of red.

When the song was over and the girls and Bones had returned to their seats, Sally realized she was gripping something in her right hand. "Stein Whatley's guitar pick," she gasped.

"Nowaynowaynoway!" Chati cheered as her fanatical friends gathered round. The rest of the concert was a fabulous blur, which Sally decided to remember as the second-best day of her life.

"The first-best day was when I met you," she whispered to Bones. The little corpse snuggled into her arms and howled in harmony with the music.

At the end of the show, Chati and her party floated out to the parking lot to wait for their respective rides.

"That was, without a doubt, the coolest concert ever," Sally said. "I mean, if this is a dream, I don't ever want to wake up!"

"I don't ever want to go home!" Chati echoed. "I could have totally danced on that stage all night."

"Me too," Sally agreed. She scanned the parking lot for her father, but his station wagon was nowhere in sight. Instead, a group of picketers across the street from the venue caught her attention. "Who are they?" Sally asked.

"Oh them? That's PAD," Chati replied. "It stands for Parents Against Death."

"Seriously?" Sally asked. "Isn't that kind of an obvious choice? Why don't they just call themselves Mammals for Breathing?"

Chati shrugged. "They show up at any event they think promotes being dead. Museum exhibits, concerts, book signings, you name it. If it's deadly, they're there."

"Really? But I've never even heard of them," Sally said, tightening the straps of Bones's carrier.

"We don't see them much in Merryland," Chati continued. "Except at concerts. There's always a new song or a group they find offensive. Just last winter, my dad booked a choir of monks from the west coast to do a holiday concert. They'd just released an album that was actually decent called *Christmas from the Coast*, but someone made a mistake and printed up hundreds of posters that called it *Christmas from the Ghost*. PAD came to protest, but when they realized their mistake they stayed for the show and even waited at the stage door for the monks' autographs. My dad says they're harmless, so he lets them picket across the street."

Though Sally wanted nothing more than to believe Chati's representation of PAD, she couldn't help but feel uneasy about a group of people who took issue with dead things. When Viola chimed in, Sally's unease became deep concern.

"Harmless here," Viola said.

"Huh?" Sally asked.

"They're harmless here, Sally," Viola repeated, addressing her enemy for the first time. "I saw some of their protests when I lived in Watta City, and wow! Let me tell you, there was nothing harmless about those mob scenes."

"Oh, no?" Sally tried to ask nonchalantly, though she knew the quiver in her voice betrayed her rising anxiety.

"Oh, yes," Viola replied, her eyes sparkling. "I've seen them come out in the thousands. When they find something that really glorifies death, they stop at nothing to bring it down." Viola glanced at Bones's carrier, out of which two wide black eyes peeked. "Sure, PAD's local chapter isn't anything to have nightmares about, but I bet all their big city members would come for a visit if they got wind of something really deadly. Or really *dead.*"

Sally gulped loudly. She felt so exposed. Where was her father? Why was he so late? She suddenly wanted nothing more than to get Bones back to the safety of her own home, lock him in her room, and protect him, just like her father had told her to from the start. She looked back at the protesters and could have sworn one of them was waving at her. Just as she was about to make a run for it, she heard three beeps and caught sight of her father's station wagon pulling into the lot.

"There's my dad." Sally's sigh was heavy with relief. "Guess Bones and I should get going. Does anyone need a ride? Seems like everyone's parents are running late." Sally smiled politely at the gang, but Chati, Susannah, and the others looked away. Viola, on the other hand, not only matched Sally's grin but raised her a chuckle.

"Oh, no, Sally. It's just my mom who's late," she cooed sweetly. "We're all riding together. You're the only one waiting for someone else to pick you up."

"Viola!" Chati gasped.

"What, Chati?" Viola snapped. "It's not like she minds." She turned to Sally. "Everyone's coming to my house for an after-party. That is, everyone except you. We didn't think you'd want to come."

Suddenly all thoughts of PAD were lost. The anxiety she had felt seemed fictional and baseless. All she could think of now was that, once again, she was being left out.

"Oh, uh, right, sure. Why would I?" Sally said. She tried in vain to maintain her own cheery smile.

"It's just that we never really see you hang out outside of school," Chati explained. "So Viola thought, and we just assumed..."

"No, no. It's okay," Sally lied. "Thanks for the concert, Chati. It was really great. Happy birthday, again." Sally turned to the station wagon, ready to make a run for it, but Chati stopped her.

"Sally, wait," Chati commanded. "Why don't you come with us to Viola's? We'd love to have you."

"What?" Viola rushed over. "No! I mean, my mother's only expecting five of us."

Chati looked at her friend, politely trying to mask her confusion at Viola's rudeness. "But I'm sure she wouldn't mind including—"

"And we can't have that dog in our house," Viola added hastily. "Princess Poopsy would freak. Sorry, Sally. It just won't work." Viola smiled insincerely while Chati looked truly dejected.

Whether it was the high of the concert returning to her or the encouragement she felt at Chati's efforts to include her, Sally decided to speak up. "We could, um, all go to my house," she said, spontaneously offering to host her very first sleepover.

"What? Why?" Viola snapped.

"So we can all hang out together and no one has to be left out," Sally replied, her voice growing stronger. "I mean, I don't have a whole party set up, but we have sleeping bags, and I could order a pizza." She smiled at Chati. "And I have a ton of Tone Death special edition CDs we could listen to all night."

Chati squealed and clapped her hands. "Omigosh, Sally, that is the bestest idea ever!"

"But what about my house?" Viola demanded.

Chati took Viola's hands in hers. "You said yourself we couldn't have Bones there. And you always have us over to your house," she reasoned. "Let Sally have a turn. I'm sure it'll be a relief to your mom, anyway." Squeezing Sally's arm, she added, "I'll go tell the girls." Chati skipped over to the rest of her party to fill everyone in.

Viola glared at Sally.

"Listen, Viola," Sally began. "You're more than welcome to—"

"Save it, Simplesmith," Viola fumed. "I wouldn't go to your house if there was an earthquake and it was the last place standing. Enjoy tonight, because soon this will all be over. I told you not to cross me. Now you're going to be sorry. Now you're going to—"

"Viola, stop," Sally interrupted. The mean girl gasped. Sally held her ground. "I won't let you scare me. Not anymore. I really don't want to be your enemy, but I won't be your whipping girl either. We need to find a way to live together, especially now that we have the same friends."

"Friends?" Viola snorted, loading up with fresh ammunition. "Oh, you have got to be kidding me. You're still a freak, Sally, now there's just a show attached. But go ahead, embrace this new cult of your personality. Just remember, the higher you climb, the farther you'll fall."

A car horn blew. Vivienne Vanderperfect stood beside her top-of-the-line SUV, which she had parked next to Mr. Simplesmith's slightly rusted station wagon. The two old friends seemed to be chatting up a storm. Seymour smiled at Vivienne as she waved to Viola and her friends.

"Ready?" Chati asked both girls when she returned.

"You know, I think I'm going to skip the slumber party tonight," Viola announced.

"Oh, no, Viola, you can't!" Chati exclaimed, distraught.

"I am super tired, and I just realized I have a ton to do tomorrow. It's really better if I get a good night's sleep so I can conquer it all in the morning." She glared at Sally. "You girls have a great time at Sally's without me."

"If you're sure," Chati wavered.

"Positive," Viola confirmed. She hugged each of the girls good-bye, finishing with Sally. Holding her in a tight embrace, Viola whispered, "I told you if you crossed me it'd be your funeral. Now your time is up."

Releasing her prey, Viola sauntered over to her mother, who was in the middle of a spirited conversation with Mr. Simplesmith.

"Well, wasn't that clever of you, Seymour," Sally heard Vivienne say with a giggle as she and the rest of the girls arrived at the parked cars. "Not that I'm surprised. You always were the best at finding unlikely solutions to absurd problems. We'll have to get together soon so I can hear more about it!" As she returned to the driver's seat of her car, she offered Sally a quick wave. "And hello–good-bye to you too, Sally! Kiss kiss!"

Sally blushed as Mrs. Vanderperfect blew kisses at the air and smiled at her with more warmth than she thought Viola would ever be capable of. But the color drained from Sally's cheeks when she saw Vivienne's reaction to all the girls turning away from her beautiful SUV and piling into Seymour's old wagon. Though Viola remained perfectly poised in the passenger's seat as she explained the sleepover shuffle to her mother, Sally felt a pang of regret thanks to the look of disappointment on Mrs. Vanderperfect's face. But it was the brave, friendly smile Viola's mother gave Sally as they drove away that truly broke her heart.

Chapter 11

On the first day of school after her slumber party, Sally entered the building braced for Viola's attack. Her entire weekend had been spent imagining horrifying scenarios, each worse than the next. Sally knew that she had never asked for this. All she ever wanted was a friend. But with each new waking nightmare came the same crystal-clear revelation: though she might not deserve Viola's cruelty, she wasn't going take it lying down. Sally would field anything Viola threw at her, and she would not go down without a knock-down, drag-out, kicking-and-screaming fight.

Unfortunately, Viola's wartime tactic was something Sally was entirely unprepared for. The armor she built was useless. The strategies she laid out, irrelevant. Viola's attack was brilliant, and had she not been so utterly unraveled by it, Sally might even have been impressed. To Sally's shock, terror, and awe, Viola Vanderperfect did the one thing she would never have imagined: absolutely nothing.

On Monday, Viola completely avoided her nemesis, finding clever ways to pass unnoticed in the halls. On

Tuesday, she made a point of ignoring Sally, refusing to make eye contact when their paths did cross. But by the end of the week, the teenaged terrorist had actually acknowledged Sally on one occasion. And after ten days of shared lunch periods, Viola seemed resigned to her enemy's presence in her social circle, even addressing Sally directly in conversation twice.

By the time one month had passed, Sally was a complete wreck. If Viola had come at her directly, Sally could have handled it. She would have fought back, with truth and justice on her side. But the anticipation was killing her. Not knowing when Viola was going to strike or what she was truly plotting behind those arctic-blue eyes quickly became too much for Sally to bear.

She began missing school, and when she was there, she made regular visits to the nurse's office. When she was not in class, Bones was always at her side, but they played less and less. The anonymous notes had stopped altogether now, but even that was little comfort to Sally. It was all about Viola.

Sally wanted only to hurry home each day, lock the front door tight, and barricade herself in her room until it was time for dinner. Late evenings were spent listening to depressing emo-pop-rock until, mercifully, it was time for bed.

It was on a Thursday, almost five weeks after Viola's silent war had begun, when Bones seemed finally to have had enough. He was trotting behind a pitifully plodding Sally when he spotted their archenemy loitering beneath a cherry tree. Before Sally knew it, Bones had charged over to Viola and was giving her a piece of his mind.

"Grwoof Rara...Rararara...Rara...Ra," Bones said as Sally scooped him up in her arms.

"Bones, stop!" she pleaded. "Viola, I'm so sorry. I don't know what's gotten into him."

"It's OK," Viola said, and she turned to enter the school.

"What do you mean, 'it's OK'?" Sally asked. Her voice cracked, and she realized she was on the verge of tears. "Please, Viola, can you stop doing this? Can't we just get it over with?"

The beautiful bully looked at Sally with convincing confusion. "Get what over with? Sally, I have no idea what you're talking about."

"Of course you do," Sally hollered in exasperation. "Why haven't you exacted your revenge already? Destroy me, make me miserable, pay me back for all the terrible things you think I've done. Just please do it now, because waiting has been torture. I don't care whether I deserve it or not, I just want it over with." She looked Viola squarely in the eye. "Here I am. Come and get me."

At first, Viola regarded Sally with uneasy disbelief. Then, quite suddenly, she began to laugh. "Do you mean to tell me that for over a month you've been totally stressed out, thinking I was plotting some huge punishment?"

"Well...yes?" Sally answered, suddenly unconvinced.

"And all this time, I was actually making an effort to leave you alone. To *not* let *you* bother *me*; to give up on putting you in your place. Ha!" she crowed. "Isn't that just the funniest thing you've ever heard?"

"Yeah," said Sally. "Hilarious."

Viola shook her head. "Listen, I can't imagine I'm ever going to like you, but I'm not sure I have the energy to bring you down either. I'm busy enough being beautiful and popular. So, I think I'd like to put the past behind us. Let's move on with our lives. What do you say?"

Sally contemplated Viola's proposal so intensely that her eyebrows nearly touched. "You're really going to leave me alone?" she asked.

"Leave. You. Alone." Viola emphasized each word. "Yes. Now, if we can consider the hatchet buried, I have to make a stop before class. See you in homeroom?"

"Sure," said Sally. "See you there."

Viola hurried off, and Sally walked Bones to the schoolyard in silence, completely lost in thought. "I don't know, boy," she finally said. "I just can't shake the feeling that that was too easy."

Bones stiffened and refused to take another step.

"You think I'm being paranoid?"

"Gruff," he told her plainly.

"Yeah. You're probably right. I'll try to take her at her word. I mean, what other choice do I have?"

"GGGgggrrr-uff! GGGgggrrr-uff!" Bones exclaimed and spun around in two circles. Sally smiled for what seemed like the first time in ages.

"Ha ha, OK. Point taken. I guess I have been a bit of a downer lately." She scratched her dog on the top of his head and led him to a grassy area by the tire swings, not far from the shed. "Guess I'll see you back here at recess. Same bat time, same bat channel?"

"GGGgggrrr-uff!" he agreed and lay down, stretching out in a sunny spot. Sally relaxed her shoulders and headed into the school building. Even though she told herself not to be too trusting, she already felt lighter. She was daydreaming about a long-overdue trip to the graveyard with Bones when she knocked into Chati, who was running into class.

"Sorry, Chati. I was spacing. I didn't see you," Sally said.

"Omigosh, omigosh, Sally, have you heard?" Chati's eyes gleamed, and she shook all over. Sally knew this look well. Chati Chattercathy was like a geyser about to erupt when she had a brand-new bit of gossip. Pulling Sally over to their gathered friends, Chati blew out all the air in her lungs before taking a deep breath. Then she was off.

"So, remember how I told you that my cousin, Vani, heard from our granny, Nanny, who was talking to the Fooleries, who knew about it from Greenly Thumb, who is best friends with Officer Stu, that someone has been stealing all the neighborhood dogs' bones?"

"Duh," said Susannah. "Everyone knows about the bone snatcher. There isn't a dog in Merryland who isn't totally whacked-out."

"Well, guess what?" Chati paused for effect. "They finally know who did it!"

The girls gasped in unison.

"Good day to be a dog," said Danny Boi, who had been eavesdropping.

"You should know," Chati cracked before shooing him away with her hands.

"No, I'm serious," Danny continued. "My dog's been going nuts, snapping at everyone. It's like he looks at me and all he sees is a supersized boy-shaped bone." A shiver ran through his body. "Even my brothers are freaked, and they're not afraid of anything."

Chati patted Danny on the shoulder. "It has been a trial for our pets, hasn't it? Speaking of trials, do you think they'll have one?" Chati clapped her hands at the thought of it. "Omigosh that would be the most exciting thing to happen in Merryland since, well, since Viola moved back."

Sally would have rolled her eyes at this comment, but she was too interested in discovering the true identity of the thief. "So who did it?" she asked.

Chati frowned. "I don't have that information right now. Vani didn't think to ask. She's not as thorough as I am. She has so much to learn. But she did find out that they'd been tracking the suspect for a while, and early this morning they caught a big break." Chati tilted her head thoughtfully. "It still just seems so random. I mean, why would anybody steal from poor innocent puppies? What does someone need with a bunch of animal bones, anyway?"

"That's a very good question, Chati," a sweet voice singsonged. Viola arrived in the doorway and glided over to her prattling peers. "I would assume that whoever took the bones really needed them for some incredibly important reason. To the thief, maybe it was a matter of life and death." She turned to Sally and, in her most innocent voice, asked, "What do you think, Sally?"

"About what?"

"Well, who do you think would need so many bones? And why is this suddenly happening now? I mean, if I were going to steal something super necessary to my existence I might stock up on lip gloss...or blood." Viola put her finger to her lips and looked off into the distance. "Come to think of it, timing is as much a question as motive. Who showed up right around the same time that all those bones went missing? And who do we know that is made entirely of bones and quite possibly needs new ones to survive?"

A fist of nausea punched Sally hard in the gut. She stumbled over to her desk and steadied herself. Though her vision was beginning to blur, she forced herself to focus when she noticed the edge of a white envelope sticking out of her desk. She tore it open and, with shaking hands, read the note.

Fool me once, shame on you.
Fool me twice, shame on you too!
And just to be sure you don't get me again
Today I destroy both you and your friend!

"No!" Sally gasped and sprinted from her classroom, down the hall, and out the side doors to the playground. There, in the grassy knoll beside the tire swings, was Bones, facing off against the D.C., who was charging at him with the long rod with the metal collar attached to its tip.

"Stop it!" Sally shrieked. "He didn't do anything! Leave him alone!"

At the sound of her voice, Bones turned, letting his guard down for only a moment. The D.C. snapped the collar around the dog's neck. "Gotcha, you little thief!"

"Ow-wooh-wooh-wooh," Bones howled, and Sally ran to him.

"Let him go," she commanded as she tried, in vain, to unlatch the collar.

"Not this time, girly," the D.C. snarled. "This mutt has committed a crime, so now he's mine."

"But he didn't do it!" Sally cried. By now, a crowd had gathered in the schoolyard.

"It's an open and shut case. Neighborhood dogs' bones start to go missing not long after a dog made of bones shows up in town. Seems perfectly clear to me." The D.C. turned to Bones and sucked his teeth. "I'm gonna take you apart, bone by bone, and give each unhappy pooch a piece of you as retribution."

Bones's eyes widened in terror, and Sally fought the urge to faint. She was scanning the crowd for someone who might help her just as Officer Stu stepped forward.

"What's going on here?"

"Officer Stu!" Sally was nearly in hysterics. "He says Bones is guilty of stealing all the other dogs' bones and that he's going to pick him apart and give a piece of him to everyone and you can't let him do that, please, you can't!"

"Oh, no, you don't," the D.C. barked. "This *thing* has violated the unalienable rights of canine citizens everywhere: to play, obey, and pursue their own happiness. He's in my jurisdiction now. And this time I've got evidence."

"Evidence?" Sally asked through her tears. "What evidence?"

The D.C. dragged Bones down the alley off the schoolyard, toward the secret shed. Sally, Officer Stu, and the gathered crowd followed.

"Got a call early this morning telling me all about the little devil's demented hideout. So I came to investigate, and I found his stash!" The D.C. threw open the door to the shed, revealing a small mound of animal bones piled in the corner. Bones pulled away, disgusted. "Let's see you talk your way out of this one, kid."

"But—but it isn't possible," Sally said, still processing the reality that her dog had been set up. "He couldn't do it, he wouldn't. You must have planted the bones, or someone else did. He's innocent! Bones is innocent!" Sally pleaded.

The D.C. laughed. "Aw, innocent until proven guilty, right? Well, what do you propose we do? Give the mutt a trial?"

"That's exactly what we're going to do," said Officer Stu.

The dog catcher stopped laughing. He stared at Stu, aghast. "Why, that's ridiculous! It's a dog! Who would defend him?"

"Me," Sally announced.

"And you can prosecute," Stu told the D.C. "I'll be the judge."

"Fine," the superior little man agreed. "I've got witnesses aplenty. People who can prove this doggie's a delinquent. He won't get away from me this time. This menacing mongrel's going down!"

Officer Stu sighed. "Well,

then, we'll meet here after school lets out tomorrow and decide the matter."

Sally turned to hug the policeman. "Oh, thank you, Officer—"

"Wait, Sally. I want to make sure you understand." Stu's eyes were sad, but his tone was stern. "Bones has been accused of a very real crime. I hope he's innocent, but I'll be honest, it isn't looking very good. Prepare your case, and I'll hear both sides tomorrow. As for Bones, he'll have to stay in the pound tonight."

"What? No!" Sally yelped. The D.C. smiled smugly.

"I'm sorry, but that's how it's got to be," Officer Stu replied. "But he'd better be well cared for and in one piece when we meet up again," he added, wiping the smile from the D.C.'s troll-like face. "Sally, say good-bye to Bones and then get back into class."

"But..." Sally whimpered. Stu held his ground.

Sally knelt down beside Bones. She held him tight. When she felt his tiny body shiver against hers, she could hold back the tears no longer. She wept as she kissed her frightened puppy.

Bones tried to be brave, but when the D.C. pulled him away from Sally, he howled and fought mightily to twist himself free. Sally lurched toward her dog, but Officer Stu held her back. Though it was a warm embrace, Sally struggled against it, knocking against Stu's chest with her shoulders and kicking wildly with her gangly legs. When she finally quieted, Stu loosened his grip and Sally stood frozen in place.

She watched, through blurred vision, as the dog catcher locked Bones in a reinforced cage and loaded him into the back of his van. The best friends stared at each other until the back doors were shut. The D.C. turned the ignition and started to pull away. "Bones!" Sally shouted, and she ran after the van.

She could hear her dog's howling long after the cold, white vehicle had driven out of sight.

Chapter 12

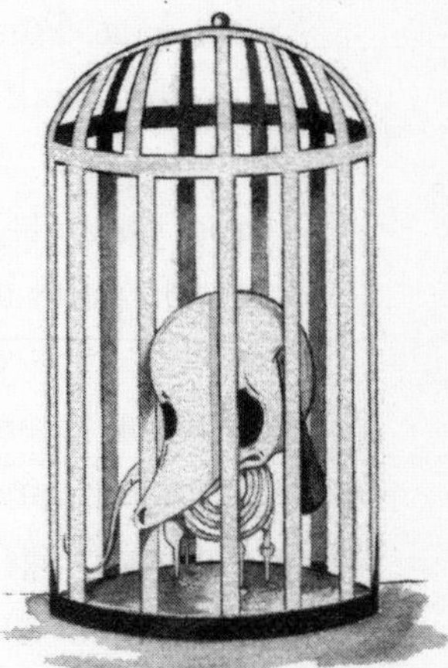

"AND THAT WAS WHEN I realized Mr. President was depressed." A heavyset woman in an orange floral muumuu dabbed at her eyes with a handkerchief and then did the same to the little dachshund on her lap.

"Depressed because he was no longer in possession of his marrow-filled bone," the D.C. clarified, oozing with greasy sympathy. "And did you look for Mr. President's missing bone?"

"Of course I did," Judy Punch replied. "Not only was it nowhere to be found, but while I was looking, I ran into Mick Barbi with his Australian terrier, G'day, and Mary Scribbler with her Plott hound, Dénouement. They were on bone hunts too!" She leaned toward Officer Stu, who sat, gavel in hand, at a picnic table next to the makeshift witness box—a child-sized chair surrounded by six milk crates, courtesy of the cafeteria.

"That was when I knew something didn't smell right. And it wasn't the kitty litter, if you know what I mean."

The crowd that had assembled on the playground of Merryland Middle School laughed heartily at Miss Punch's joke. Officer Stu banged his gavel and called for order.

"Now, Miss Punch. You believe you know who the culprit is, don't you?" The D.C. glared at Sally as he asked the question.

"I most certainly do," she righteously replied.

"Can you point him out to us?"

"Yes. It's that demon doggie there!" Judy Punch pointed at the canine skeleton imprisoned in the dome-shaped monkey bars. The audience gasped as Officer Stu banged his gavel again.

"And how do you know that animal is guilty, Miss Punch?" the D.C. asked.

"You mean aside from just looking at him? Well, the very same night I realized Mr. President's bone had been picked, I saw the accused digging in the yard across the street. I'd bet that if you excavate there, you'll find all the missing bones!"

The D.C. sneered at Sally. "Your witness."

The previous morning, after her dog had been arrested and carted off, Sally had sobbed in the schoolyard for a full, uninterrupted seven and a half minutes. Then she dried her eyes and returned to class. Chati Chattercathy offered her heartfelt sympathies and a shoulder on which to cry some more, but Sally politely declined.

"The time for tears is over," she had said. "I've got a trial to prepare for." And prepare she did; all that afternoon, through the evening and well into the night. Standing before her first witness, Sally felt calm. She was going to eat this woman for lunch.

"Hi, Miss Punch," Sally began.

"Hi, Sally, honey," the witness replied cheerily.

"I'm very sorry for Mr. President's loss."

"Thank you, darling." Miss Punch touched her hand to her heart. "That's very kind of you."

"No problem." Sally smiled. "So, um, you say that the evidence you have against my client is that you saw him digging in the yard across the street on the same night as the suspected theft. Is that correct?"

"Well, yes. That and the fact that he's just plain creepy! I mean, honestly, who else could it be?"

The crowd mumbled in agreement.

"Right." Sally nodded politely. "But, removing that second part of your statement, which is speculation and therefore not factual evidence, the only reason you have to suspect Bones is because you saw him near the crime scene, aka your house, on that fateful night?"

"Well, yes. I suppose so." Miss Punch shifted in her seat.

"Miss Punch, where do you live?"

"At 1445 Pinecrest Drive."

"Miss Punch, where do I live?"

The witness snickered. "Well, right across the street from me, Sally, or did you forget?" The crowd chuckled. Sally laughed along.

"No, ma'am, I didn't." She turned to Bones and winked. "So, if you live across the street from me and, presumably, it was my yard in which you saw Bones digging, wouldn't it stand to reason that he was digging not to hide his loot but because he was simply being a dog, playing on his own property?"

As the assembled onlookers discussed this new scenario, Sally shouted over them. "I'd like to introduce into evidence Defense Exhibit A: a photograph of our backyard that shows not the fresh mounds of dirt one would associate with something newly buried, but hole upon hole of dug-up earth in which it would be impossible to hide one, let alone dozens of bones." Sally addressed the crowd. "If Bones is guilty of anything, it's destroying my father's garden. Your honor, I am through with this witness."

Miss Punch left the witness stand, and the D.C. glowered at Sally. "Don't worry, girly. I've got plenty more where that one came from," he hissed as she walked past.

"Bring 'em on, I'll knock 'em down," Sally replied in her own low growl.

Much of the afternoon followed in the same manner. The D.C. would provide a witness who was convinced of Bones's guilt, and Sally would show that his or her accusation wasn't based on fact, but on prejudice. After an hour of such back-and-forth, the crowd was clearly getting restless, and Sally was feeling slightly bored.

"The prosecution calls Vivienne Vanderperfect to the stand."

Mrs. Vanderperfect sauntered over to the milk crates, smiling at Sally as she passed her.

"Do you swear to tell the truth, the whole truth, and nothing but the truth?" Officer Stu asked.

"Well, of course!" Vivienne responded brightly. The charmed audience sighed.

"Mrs. Vanderperfect, do you know why you've been called as a witness today?" the D.C. asked.

"I'd imagine it's because I reported that my beautiful daughter's prize-winning poodle was a victim of this horrible bone-stealing crime," Vivienne answered.

"Not just any victim, ma'am, but the very first victim!" the trollish little man declared. "When did you report the theft?"

"Well, let me see," Vivienne considered. "I first reported it the night of Viola's birthday party, September twenty-ninth."

"The first night anyone other than the Simplesmith family caught sight of the accused!" the D.C. shouted triumphantly. Vivienne looked to Sally, perplexed.

"Yes, I suppose that's true, but that was just a coincidence," she explained. "You see, Princess Poopsy's bones had started to go missing a bit before that, just about a month. I simply hadn't noticed because, well," she giggled to herself, "Poopsy has so many bones I sometimes lose track."

The crowd laughed politely at Vivienne's adorable embarrassment of riches while the D.C. prepared his attack.

"Princess Poopsy's bones started to go missing almost a month before your daughter's birthday, you say? Talk about a coincidence!" He turned toward Sally, though he continued to address the witness. "That would put the first theft at right about the same time that demon dog arrived in Merryland! As Officer Stu himself knows, Bones Simplesmith's recorded rebirth date is September first!"

The stunned onlookers could not keep quiet. Officer Stu banged his gavel as Sally took in the crowd. At the front of the audience sat her father, pinching his fingers and adjusting his glasses as he studied the proceedings. Beside him was a small group of Sally's supporters, lead by Chati Chattercathy and Susannah Oh. Across the way was a gathering of PAD protestors, holding pickets signs with slogans like "Death to Death" and "Give a dog a BONES!" And flanking the sides of the gathering was an assortment of frustrated dog owners and their victimized pups. Though the animals were, for the most part, on their best behavior, Sally didn't like the crazed looks in their eyes or the way they drooled whenever they caught a glimpse of Bones.

"One final question, Mrs. Vanderperfect," the D.C.

shouted over the crowd, snapping everyone back to attention. "Would you please reveal to us the identity of the criminal mastermind behind these bone thefts?"

"I'd be happy to," Vivienne replied, as pleasantly as ever. Sally slumped in her seat, fearing the worst. "But I'm sorry to say I can't."

Sally bolted upright as the D.C. glared at his witness.

"What was that?" the D.C. asked.

"I'm sure many people will point their fingers at the creature in the monkey-bar jail over there, but I'm sorry, I just can't tell you without a doubt that he is the one who did it. I would if I had seen him with my own two eyes, but I didn't. I took an oath to answer your questions truthfully, and that's all any of us can be expected to do."

Sally regarded the prosecution's witness in appreciation and amazement.

"Sally, do you have any questions for this witness?" Officer Stu asked.

"No, I don't," she replied. "I think Mrs. Vanderperfect has said it all."

Vivienne Vanderperfect stepped down from the witness stand, and Sally smiled at the woman who really had been her mother's friend.

At Officer Stu's request, Sally and the D.C. approached the bench. "Does the prosecution have any other witnesses, preferably ones who can speak directly to the accused's guilt?" Sally stifled a giggle as the D.C. growled.

"One final witness," he replied. "The prosecution calls Thomas Gunn."

Sally no longer felt like laughing. Why would the D.C. call Tommy? While she knew they had had their differences, she hadn't expected him to play for the other side. As Tommy took the stand, he kept his eyes trained on the ground. Sally heard a small cheer break out from the crowd. One of the PAD protestors was waving at Tommy. Sally shook her head in disbelief. It was his mom.

"Mr. Gunn, can you tell us about a particular fight you and the accused's owner had during recess a few months back?"

Tommy shrugged. "I wouldn't exactly call it a fight."

The D.C. clarified, "Disagreement, then. When did it happen, and what was it about?"

Tommy stared at Sally for a long time without saying a word. She glared back at him until he finally looked away.

"It was the first day back at school after Skeletor, I mean, Bones, showed up at Viola Vanderperfect's birthday party," Tommy explained. "I'd seen Sally arguing with you and Officer Stu earlier that morning and when I asked her about it, she freaked out."

"Freaked out?" the D.C. asked. "How exactly did she 'freak out'?"

"She yelled at me for getting her dumb dog's name wrong and then told me to get lost." Tommy looked to Sally again. "I wasn't trying to make her mad. I just wanted to be nice." The audience *aww*ed. Sally began to get scared.

"But if you were just being nice, Tommy, wouldn't you say that Miss Simplesmith's reaction had nothing to do with your actions and must have been because she was on edge trying to cover up her companion's crimes? Couldn't it be that she was taking her stress out on you?"

The audience leaned in, waiting for Tommy's accusation. Sally glanced back at Mrs. Gunn, who was hugging her picket sign and nodding to her son encouragingly. Somehow, Tommy Gunn had become an incredibly sympathetic witness for the prosecution.

"Maybe," he finally replied. "But I wouldn't know for sure, because when I went to find her later at the garbage shed where we sometimes hang out—"

"Wha-what did you say?" the D.C. asked, flummoxed.

"I said I went looking for her at the garbage shed that we all know about and can go to any time we want." Tommy glanced quickly at Sally, who could have sworn she saw him wink.

"No further questions for this witness," the D.C. muttered quickly. "He's dismissed."

Though the gathered crowd had not yet caught on, Sally understood exactly the opening Tommy had just given her.

"Wait, I have a question," she said before Tommy had

moved from his seat. "Tommy, you said that everyone knew about the garbage shed where Bones and I sometimes hung out, correct?"

"Yep," he replied, coolly.

"So if everyone knew about it, anyone could have gone to it at any time, correct?"

"Yep."

"Therefore it stands to reason that anyone who knew about it and had access to it could have put the stolen bones there, thus making the D.C.'s assertion that the stolen bones found in the shed could only have belonged to Bones incorrect. Correct?"

Tommy hit his forehead with the heel of his palm. "Gosh, I guess you're right. I suppose anyone who knew about the shed could have been the real bone snatcher. Maybe it wasn't Bones after all."

"Thank you, Tommy," Sally said, and she meant it. "This witness is dismissed."

As Tommy left the stand, the crowd heatedly discussed his testimony. Realizing he wouldn't quiet them any time soon, Officer Stu called a ten-minute recess.

"I'd like to wrap this up," he told counsel as he headed inside the school for a bathroom break. "And I'd prefer not to have any more unreliable testimony about Bones's guilt or reference to the pile of bones found in an obviously public shed. Let's hear some new evidence, or let's go home."

The D.C. stomped away, muttering words to himself that Sally was sure she was too young to hear. Though she tried to temper her elation, fully aware that the trial had not yet been won, she couldn't resist skipping a little as she headed over to give her client a hug.

Chapter 13

"YOU'RE DOING GREAT, SAL," Mr. Simplesmith said as he greeted his daughter at the monkey-bar jail.

"Thanks, Dad." Sally smiled. She pet her incarcerated pup, who wiggled and wagged in delight. "I just want this whole nightmare to be over."

"Oh, I'm sure you do, you poor dear!" Vivienne Vanderperfect said as she appeared at Seymour's side. Viola slogged behind her.

"Well hey there, Viv." Mr. Simplesmith smiled. "Wasn't that nice of Viola and her mom to come out and show their support, Sally?"

"It really was," Sally agreed. "Thanks so much for your testimony, Mrs. Vanderperfect."

"Now, I told you to call me Vivienne, darling!" Viola's mother reminded. "And no thanks are necessary. I simply answered that man's questions. I have faith that things will turn out right in the end."

Sally beamed at Vivienne, and for her sake tried hard not to glare at Viola, who refused to look up from her newly manicured nails.

"I just think it's so terrible that you have to go through this. And you, Seymour," Vivienne took his hand. "I'm sure it was hard enough when Sally brought home that…well, 'dog' is probably the wrong word. But to agree to house him and then have him turn on you like that? Such a shame."

"But Bones is innocent, Mrs. Vanderperfect," Sally declared, shocked that the same woman who had just given such helpful testimony was actually suspicious.

"Of course he is, honey," Vivienne humored.

"No, it's true," Sally insisted. "He doesn't even like bones!"

Viola looked up. "How can he not like them? He's made out of them."

"No, I mean he doesn't like chewing on them. He thinks it's repulsive," Sally explained. "That's how I know he didn't do what he's accused of. It would gross him out too much." Sally waited for some sort of apology from Viola and her mother, but Viola merely shrugged as Mrs. Vanderperfect indulged Sally with an exaggerated expression of concern. Sally was preparing to explain again when her father spoke.

"But Sal," Mr. Simplesmith said uneasily. "Don't you remember the chicken bone, that first night?"

Officer Stu returned to the picnic bench and called the court to order.

"What?" Sally asked, surprised.

"The first night you brought Bones home, I gave him a chicken bone. And, well, don't you remember honey? He took it."

Sally pulled her father away from the Vanderperfects. "Oh, yeah, that," she mumbled as Stu's gavel banged for the fourth time. "Look, Dad, I can't explain now, but not everything is exactly how it looks. I'll fill you in later, but please keep the chicken bone to yourself and trust me. I swear Bones didn't do this, all right?"

"But—"

"Daddy. Please."

Mr. Simplesmith hovered for a moment but said nothing more and returned, perplexed, to his seat. Sally looked at Bones through the monkey bars. "You ready, boy?"

"GGGgggrrr-uff!" he replied. Sally smiled at him proudly.

"Court is now in session," Officer Stu announced. "Does the prosecution have any other witnesses?"

"Not at this time," the D.C. grumbled. Sally felt her heart skip.

"Sally, is there anyone you'd like to call to the stand?"

"Yes, Officer Stu, there is. I would like to call the defendant, Bones Simplesmith."

Bones was released from the monkey-bar jail and led to the witness box. The majority of the onlookers glared and growled at him as he paraded past. The confused canine dropped his ears and tucked his tail. He looked at Sally, who offered him her most comforting smile as she guided him to the chair behind the milk crate.

"Now, Bones," Sally began. "I will make this brief. Since you can't speak, please just reply in the affirmative or negative to each question asked. Are you one Bones Simplesmith?"

"GGGgggrrr-uff." The incarcerated carcass spun around in a circle.

"Thank you." Sally proceeded. "Are you guilty of the crime brought against you? Did you steal all the neighborhood dogs' bones?"

"Grwof," Bones replied. He placed his front paws on a milk carton and lowered his chin on top of them.

"If it please the court, I'd like to do a demonstration that will prove why my client could never have committed this cruel crime." Sally motioned to Chati Chattercathy, who stepped forward with a brown paper bag.

"Thanks, Chati." Sally smiled at her friend. She was wearing a homemade "Free Bones" button, and Sally had to force down the lump in her chest that had grown out of Chati's kindness. She cleared her throat.

"In this bag, I have two items. One of them Bones loves, while the other, he detests more than anything else in the world." Sally handed Officer Stu the bag. "If you'd please pull out one item and offer it to Bones, you can judge his reaction for yourself."

Officer Stu reached his hand into the bag. He pulled out a plush toy bone and waved it in front of the little cadaver. Bones panted and wiggled and wagged excitedly.

"GGGgggrrr-uff! GGGgggrrr-uff!" he yapped. He jumped out of the witness box and onto the picnic table. He grabbed the toy in his teeth. The crowd tittered at the joyous display.

"Officer Stu," Sally continued, "please offer Bones the other item."

Stu reached into the brown paper bag and produced a juicy, marrow-filled bone, fresh from the local butcher. Instantly, Bones froze. His tail stilled, and he dropped the plush toy from his mouth. He made gagging noises before rebuking Officer Stu with a resounding, "Grwof!" Turning his back on both the toy bone and the real one, Bones stomped over to the witness box and sat. The wounded animal refused to look in the lawman's direction.

"Let the record show that the accused could not have stolen the neighborhood dogs' bones because he is disgusted by them. In addition to having no motive, Bones would never have allowed himself to touch one in the first place!" Sally slammed her fist on the picnic table and shouted, "I call for an immediate dismissal of this shameful case!"

The assembled spectators erupted. The D.C.'s shouting was impossible to make out over all the noise, and Officer Stu's banging gavel barely made a sound. Sally picked up the two bones with which she had made her case and placed them back in the paper bag. She walked to the witness box and sat on a milk crate next to Bones. "I think it's over," she whispered. The dead dog smiled.

In the general confusion, it took Sally a few moments to realize that the D.C. was demanding to call another witness.

"You've already called your witnesses," Officer Stu hollered over the intensifying din.

"But I just found out what this witness knows. I only have two questions for…" The D.C. paused for effect. "Seymour Simplesmith!"

The crowd immediately fell silent. Sally's father apprehensively stepped forward. "Me?" he asked. "What do you want to know from me?"

The D.C. wasted no time, rattling off his questions before Seymour could even make it to the stand. "Are you the defendant's owner's guardian?"

"Well, I'm Sally's father, so I guess that's a yes." Seymour looked questioningly at Sally, who shrugged.

"So you've known the defendant since your daughter brought him home," the D.C. submitted.

"Sure."

"Then you must have known that the accused hates

bones, that he would never ever touch one himself. Tell me, Mr. Simplesmith. Is it true?" The D.C. waited.

"Oh, well, um..." Seymour stalled. Sally felt her entire body tense.

"I'm sorry, was that question too hard? How about this: Your daughter swears that the defendant could not have committed the crime of which he is accused because he absolutely detests touching real bones. But tell us, Mr. Simplesmith, haven't you seen him chew one?"

The entire crowd held its breath. Sally's father mopped his brow with his sleeve. He looked to his daughter, who was silently begging him to ignore his data just this once, to trust her, to lie. For all Seymour knew, Bones had enjoyed the chicken bone he had been offered their first night together. Sally had forced Bones to lie so that Seymour would accept him. She had never trusted her father with the truth, and now she watched, helpless, as he struggled between his paternal instinct to help his daughter and his scientific responsibility to trust the facts.

Mr. Simplesmith looked at the ground. "I'm so sorry, Sal," was all she heard of her father's confession before the crowd was on its feet, roaring for a guilty verdict.

Sally looked at Officer Stu as he banged his gavel and shouted for order. She saw the D.C. turn red as he screamed for an immediate judgment. She watched her father, unable to look at her, nervously pinching his thumbs. She surveyed the audience of her bloodthirsty neighbors and their maniacal mutts. Then she looked at Bones, so small and helpless, boxed in by a half dozen milk crates. He tilted his head and looked up at her with empty black eyes. Leaning toward her hand, he gave it a single lick.

Looking back, Sally would never remember the first few steps she took toward freedom. It was only when she was running from the schoolyard with a liberated Bones in her arms that she even realized what she had done.

Sally Simplesmith was a fugitive.

Chapter 14

"FOUR TWENTY-FIVE, FOUR FIFTY, four sixty, four sixty-five." Sally regarded the money in her left hand. "All we've got is a lousy four dollars and sixty-five cents to start our new life on the lam." She closed her fist around the cash. "We are so totally toast."

Bones and Sally sat in a large abandoned drainpipe on the outskirts of town. Her first instinct had been to hide at the cemetery, until she realized it would be the first place the police would look. She couldn't go home, and school was off limits. She didn't have a single friend she was sure wouldn't turn her in, and how could she blame them? Her own father had just stabbed her in the back.

The old waterworks was the only place Sally thought they might be safe, at least for tonight. The fact that it was on the way to Watta City also worked in its favor. Sally hoped that there, in a city of millions, she and Bones might begin fresh. But with only $4.65 in her pocket, Sally was starting to think things might end before they could even get started. She was calculating the likelihood of becoming Tone Death's roadie when Bones began to paw at her crossed arms.

"Bones, stop," Sally said, exhausted. The little corpse continued to tug and scratch, undeterred.

"Bones, come on," she whined. "Just give me a few minutes to think." She turned away, but the dog stayed with her.

"Rarara, Grruff," he playfully yelped. He pounced on her chest, knocking her to the ground. He dug at her tightly crossed arms until Sally snapped.

"Bones, I said cut it out!" she yelled. "I need to think, to figure this out, and you're making it worse. So leave me alone, OK? Just leave me alone."

Bones froze and stared, puzzled, at his angry friend. Reluctantly he climbed off her and settled down a few feet away.

Sally lay on her back, letting tears fall from the sides of her eyes into her ears. After a good cry, she crawled over to her pet and gave him a hug.

"I'm sorry. I shouldn't have yelled at you," she whispered. Bones tilted his face up to hers and licked the salty spots where the tears had fallen. After a few minutes, he began to poke at her arm again.

"Geez Louise, Bones, what are you after?" Sally asked, and then she felt it. When they fled the schoolyard, she had been holding the paper bag with Bones's bones in it. At some point she must have stuffed the sack in her shirtsleeve and promptly forgotten about it. Now, as she produced the crumpled bag in the dank shelter of the drainpipe, Bones whined in anticipation.

"GGGgggrrr-uff!" he barked when Sally revealed the plush toy bone. Taking one end in his mouth and holding the other between his paws, he engaged in a game of tug-of-war with himself. Sally removed the other bone, the real one, from the bag and held it up to her face.

"Too bad we didn't have time to give this to one of the bone snatcher's victims," she said. Bones put down his toy and growled angrily at the cause of their troubles. In one swift motion, he knocked the bone from Sally's hand into the mud.

"Hey! What'd you do that for?" she asked.

Bones did not reply.

"Seriously, Bones, that was a total waste. We could have at least given it to a dog we met on our way to Watta City. Anything to help out our karma—or to stop an angry dog from attacking you—would be good."

Sally slumped her shoulders and rested her chin on her fist. "Whatever," she groaned. "None of it matters anymore, anyway."

Bones let out a heavy sigh. He climbed out of the drainpipe and waded into the mud, grumbling a little before focusing his attention on one puddle in particular. Sniffing around its surface, he inhaled all the smells of the marsh until he was able to isolate the one he wanted. He followed his snout in a zigzag formation until, suddenly, he froze, one paw raised and his tail sticking straight up. He shot Sally a sideways glance before plunging directly into the muck.

When he emerged, Bones held in his mouth the real-deal marrowbone. He tiptoed back over to Sally and flung it at her feet in a mixture of triumph and disgust.

"Aw, Bones." Sally smiled guiltily. "You didn't have to do that." Hugging her muddy mutt, she added, "And I'm sorry I'm so cranky. It's just that I can't believe all this is happening. I mean, if only we knew who the bad guy was, we could expose him and clear our names. There are definitely suspects."

Bones cuddled onto Sally's lap as she laid out the possibilities. "Obviously, the D.C.'s on the list. He'd be the first to set you up."

"Ggruff," Bones agreed.

"Or maybe it was one of those PAD people. If they've got a problem with dead things, I can see why they'd go after you."

Bones whimpered, his feelings hurt.

"Not that they should," Sally clarified. "But they're totally the type to protest first and get to know you later.

"And then there's Tommy Gunn. His mom's a member of PAD, and he started acting really weird the first time he saw you—suddenly trying to talk to us, asking us to hang out."

Bones stared at Sally blankly.

"All right, fine. I suppose he did actually help us out today. Maybe Tommy isn't the *worst* person in the world."

"GGGggrrruff! GGGgggrrruff!!" Bones jumped off Sally's lap and yapped excitedly. Tommy Gunn seemed to have a fan.

"Of course, there's always Viola."

Bones let out a low growl.

"But why now? She's had it in for us for so long, what was she waiting for? I just don't see it." Sally lay back and stared at the ceiling of the drainpipe. "Seriously, though, what's the point? Why even bother trying to figure out who the real bone snatcher is? It's not like we're ever going home."

Sally covered her face with her hands. "We'd probably have better luck winning the lottery. Our chances of finding the real bad guy are one in a million. Less than zero. It'd be like searching for a needle in a haystack."

Sally gasped as she shot up to a seated position. She grabbed Bones by the leg. "Or maybe it'd be like fishing a bone out of a puddle of mud!"

Bones cocked his head to one side and flicked his ears back.

"Here, smell this," Sally said, as she thrust the marrowbone into her dog's face.

"Grwof!" he reprimanded and shuffled backward. He scurried to the far end of the drainpipe.

"Bones. I'm serious. Take a good whiff. It's what the real crook is stealing—fresh marrowbones—so the stolen ones must smell something like this. If you can follow the scent to the missing bones, maybe we can catch the real thief!" Sally eagerly held out the bone. Her dog did not move.

"Please, boy," she begged. "This is our only chance to clear our names, and if we do..." Sally blinked away tears. "Then maybe we can go home."

Reluctantly, Bones inched forward. He sniffed the marrowbone thoroughly, though Sally could tell he wanted nothing more than to turn away in disgust. When he was through, he looked at her and barked.

Exiting the drainpipe, Bones put his nose to the ground. Sally followed close behind as her dog, hot on the trail, directed them back toward Merryland and, she hoped, the villain who had set them up.

Chapter 15

IT WAS A DUSKY night in Merryland. The stars twinkled dully around a crescent moon that played hide-and-seek with thick gray clouds. The muted glow of streetlights haunted sidewalks through a veil of fog. And in the shadows lurked two creatures, each hunting, each also hunted.

Sally hugged herself with straitjacketed arms, but it did little to still the shivers that afflicted her this blustery night. She followed closely behind Bones, the Sherlock to her Watson, as the canine corpse tracked the scent of real, marrow-filled bones. Three times already the trails they'd followed had gone cold; first at a butcher's shop, then in a meatpacking plant, and lastly at the pound. Sally had been hopeful that this third trail would reveal the D.C.'s private stash, but all they found were bah-humbugging hounds whose longing for a simple marrowbone made Bones seem like fresh meat.

After going at it for hours, they finally landed on a new path that had potential. It led the junior sleuths out of the town center, toward the more residential neighborhoods where many of the bone snatcher's victims lived.

They passed a small ranch-style home with peeling white paint and partially hinged shutters. The mailbox had fallen off its post and lounged lazily on its side. Behind the chain-link fence, which was rusting and bent, lay a mangy little mutt. He sniffed in the air as Bones crept by. Licking his lips, he growled.

Suddenly the dog leapt to his feet, snarling and snapping and scratching wildly at the fence. Sally fell back and shoved Bones behind her. She was sure the crazed canine would have climbed the fence, had he not been chained to a post in his yard.

"Keep moving," Sally instructed. Peeking in the front window of the dilapidated house as she and Bones hurried on, she saw Danny Boi wrestling with his brothers. Or so she thought, until she realized he was crying uncle, to the amusement of the larger boys. His parents, who watched TV in the adjacent den, did nothing to help.

"Poor Danny," Sally said. "And poor crazy dog."

"Grruff," Bones concurred without lifting his snout.

A few blocks away, Bones caught a stronger scent. On the corner of Euclid and Elm stood a moderately sized split-level with a small, open yard. A hound dog dawdled toward Sally and Bones but stopped a few feet from the property's edge.

"Invisible fence, huh, boy?" Sally smiled at the floppy-faced dog. He grumbled and plopped down, staring at Bones with wistful longing. Sally was about to give the depressed pet her one marrowbone when the door to the backyard slammed open, and Tommy Gunn barreled out. His mother, wearing a Parents Against Death jacket, charged after him, yelling. Neither wanting to see or be seen, Sally and Bones quickly turned another corner and were out of sight.

"If we ever get out of this mess, maybe we should walk home with Tommy sometime," Sally suggested. Bones wagged his tail in agreement.

As they neared the top of a beautiful, tree-lined street, they came upon a plucky little puggle that Sally instantly recognized as Peaches, Chati Chattercathy's designer mutt. "Hi, Peaches," she whispered as she leaned over the crisp white picket fence. But Peaches, who normally couldn't resist any attention, only stared at them from inside a clapboard doghouse.

"Things really are bad," Sally said to Bones. "I hate to say it, but I kind of get why all the dog owners are out for, well, bones. Their puppies need Prozac." Sally reached into the brown bag and revealed the lone marrowbone. Peaches instantly perked up. "Here you go, girl," she stage-whispered as she tossed the treat into the yard. It landed with a thud, and a light went on in an upstairs room.

Sally and Bones retreated into the shadows just as Chati appeared at her bedroom window. She shined a flashlight around the yard and dialed her cell phone.

"Mom? It's me...me, Chati...Yes, I know you're still at the show, but I heard something in the...no, of course I'm not making this up. There was a loud noise, and I don't like being here alone. I had a really long day. My friend is missing, and I...Well, how soon will you and Daddy...yes, I know you have to work, but...well, sure the alarm's on, but I'd feel a lot better if you'd just come...no, I'm sorry...OK, all right. I'll see you in the morning, and I won't bother you again unless there's an actual intruder in the...hello?" Chati hung up her phone and did one more sweep of the yard with her flashlight. She kept her bedroom light on and pulled the drapes shut.

"See you, Chati," Sally whispered, knowing her voice would not reach the second floor. She waved at the friend who could not see her as she and Bones crept from their hiding place.

As they wandered the deserted suburban streets, Sally realized how much she missed her father. She wondered where he was right now and if he was asking himself the same question about her. Probably not, she decided. He was most likely at the lab, working hard, focused on nothing but his experiments. Sally was picturing him smiling warmly at his well-behaved fruit flies when Bones picked up a fresh scent. He wagged his tail furiously and charged ahead. Sally jogged alongside him, hurrying to keep up. When he stopped abruptly, she tripped over her own feet and tumbled off the sidewalk. She landed in a heap at the foot of an elegantly paved, long, and winding drive.

Bones sat beside her, looking through the imposing front gates. She saw a fuzzy toy bone in the grass just on the other side.

"Bones, are you kidding me?" Sally fell backward and covered her face. "Did you bring us to the Vanderperfects' just to find Princess Poopsy and her stupid toy? We were in search of *real* bones, Bones, not fuzzy ones! Now we're going to have to start all over again. I can't believe we wasted all this time. I can't believe you—"

"Grwoff!" Bones interrupted. He motioned for Sally to look deeper into the yard. What she saw this time brought her to her feet. Just up the hill of the Vanderperfect Estate stood Princess Poopsy von Vanderpoodle, but she was not concerned with a plush toy bone. Instead, she was furiously digging, retrieving the one thing everyone so desperately wanted. Caked in dirt and happy as a clam, the pretty poodle popped up holding a slightly chewed marrowbone in her mouth. Sally patted Bones lightly on the head.

"By George," she whispered. "I think she's got it."

Chapter 16

SALLY REGARDED THE VANDERPERFECTS' formidable gate. It stood at least thirty feet high, and each individual rail ended in a terrifying spearhead that Sally pictured Viola sharpening twice a day, just for fun. The hinges were fastened with what looked like Frankenstein's neck bolts, and the place where the two sides came together was lined with an electrical cord that Sally imagined would give a painful shock. She turned to comment on their sorry situation, but her partner in crime was no longer by her side.

"GGGgggrrr-uff!" Bones said as he slipped through the

narrow opening between two of the rails. "Rara, Ggruff," he added, eager for her to follow.

"Seriously, Bones? Even a Hollywood starlet couldn't fit through there," said Sally. "I'll just have to find another way in." But after fifteen minutes of staring blankly at the rails, Sally worried that she might never figure out how to break or enter. Just as she was about to give up, she heard the low rumbling of an approaching car.

"Bones, hide," she commanded and ducked behind a shrub.

From her somewhat obstructed vantage point, Sally saw Officer Stu's squad car pull up to the Vanderperfects' front gate. There were two other people in the vehicle with him, but she could only make out one: the dreaded D.C.

"Oh, come on," she whispered to an unseen higher power. "Couldn't you give me even the tiniest break?" As if in answer to her prayers, the gates creaked open and the squad car headed up the drive. Once it was out of sight, Sally slipped through the gates just as they were about to close. She hurried toward the grassy area where she had instructed Bones to hide and found him curled up in a flower bed.

"Pushing up daisies, are we?" Sally joked. Bones craned his neck toward her and kissed her softly on the cheek.

"Are you ready to do this?" she asked.

"Ggruff," Bones confirmed, and he jumped to his feet.

Sticking to the shadows, the fugitives hurried up the drive. When they arrived at the Vanderperfects' house,

Vivienne was arguing with Officer Stu and his companions out front.

"Really, Officer, I don't know what more I can tell you," Mrs. Vanderperfect complained. She pointed at the D.C. "I told this gentleman that I heard Seymour say Sally was lying about that animal-thing of hers not liking real bones, and that was all. I really don't know why you're interrupting my evening for this."

"I never said Sally was lying," the previously unseen passenger interjected. "I reminded her that I had seen Bones touch a real bone once before, and she told me things weren't as they appeared." Seymour Simplesmith turned to Officer Stu. "You called court back into session before she had the chance to finish."

"What else could she say?" the D.C. hissed. "She said the dog never touched a bone, but you saw him do it. End of story."

"That is *not* the end of the story," Sally's father snapped. "And I'm sorry to interrupt your evening, Vivienne, but mine's been derailed a bit too. My daughter is missing, or haven't you heard?"

"Now, Seymour," Mrs. Vanderperfect patronized. "There's no need to take that tone with me." She put an arm around her dead friend's husband and moved him toward the squad car. "I truly am sorry that Sally has run off, but, well, let's be honest. There's always been something a bit off about your girl. She's a sad, lonely child who will do anything for attention. Why else would she bother with that hellion-hound?"

The D.C. sniggered. Vivienne continued, "Soon enough, Sally will realize he isn't going to get her the kind of spotlight she craves, so she'll dump him and come crawling back home." She helped Seymour into the passenger seat of Officer Stu's car. "I only hope your relief at her safe return will not stop you from punishing her as she deserves."

Sally was shocked. Hadn't this woman been her friend? Vivienne had always been so nice to Sally, and she was one of the only witnesses who hadn't accused Bones at the trial. Why would she turn against them now?

As Mrs. Vanderperfect returned to her house, Seymour defiantly exited the car. "Vivienne," he bellowed. She pivoted to face him, stunned by his thundering tone. "How dare you speak about my daughter like that? Sally is the best kid a parent could ever hope for, and she's had to endure more than most. She is graceful, and she is kind.

"In fact," he continued, his voice rising, "my Sally has such a big heart that she was able to love something that everyone else feared, to see the good in a helpless little animal that anyone else would have shunned. And she had the courage to protect him when people like you were calling for blood. If that makes her 'a bit off,' then that's the kind of off I can be proud of."

"Seymour, please—" Vivienne began, but Sally's father carried on.

"Now, I am not a man who wastes his time with regret, but today I am filled with it. I didn't stand up for my beautiful, smart, honest little girl when I should have. I didn't put my faith in the one person who most deserved it. But that changes now."

"Stu." Seymour addressed the honorable lawman. "I'd like to withdraw my testimony, if that's all right with you. If Sally says Bones detests bones, then he does. If she says he is innocent, then he is. And if I have to, I'll spend the rest of my life proving it."

Officer Stu nodded, and the D.C. threw his hands in the air. He headed for the squad car, but Seymour stopped him. "And you can trust me when I tell you that I am not a man you want to go up against when it comes to discovering the truth."

Sally couldn't remember ever having heard Seymour confront anyone about anything, let alone something to do with her. Happy tears filled her eyes, and she wanted nothing more than to throw her arms around her first-rate father, but before she could even consider revealing herself, someone else sprinted from the shadows and leapt into Mr. Simplesmith's arms.

"GGGgggrrrr-uff!" Bones barked, and he showered Seymour with big, wet kisses.

The stunned adults were still frozen in shock when Sally

darted past. She briefly stopped at her father, giving him a drive-by peck on the cheek. She snapped her fingers at Bones, who leapt out of Seymour's arms and ran to her side.

"I love you, Daddy!" Sally called as she raced into the Vanderperfects' house.

Chapter 17

The grand foyer was more extravagant than Sally had imagined. Two stories tall with a seven-tiered chandelier at the center, it showcased a sweeping staircase that curved along the room's perimeter and ended on a high landing to the right. Sally saw Princess Poopsy disappear into a hallway off the balcony, but as she made for the stairs, Sally lost her footing and slipped on the buffed marble floor. Bones followed suit, and the duo slid across the length of the room. They landed in a tangled heap at the entrance to the Vanderperfect's formal dining room, where Viola was waiting impatiently for her mother to return.

"Oh. My. God!" the displeased diner declared. "I thought I was rid of you. What are you doing in my house?"

Sally rose to her feet and charged at her fair-haired foe. "What do you think I'm doing here, you horrible lying thief? It's one thing not to like me but to go after an innocent animal? That is beyond mean, and I am so going to take you down."

"What are you talking about?" Viola slammed her utensils on the table. "What are you talking about?!"

Hands on her hips and justice on her side, Sally laid it out. "I know you're the real bone snatcher, Viola. I know you set us up. The night of your birthday party, you told your mom someone had been stealing Princess Poopsy's bones. You told her it'd been going on since the day we met, which, lucky for you, also happened to be the same night I found Bones. You then went around town stealing the bones of other innocent pets until you finally planted the evidence in the shed where you knew Bones and I hung out. Then you called the D.C. and tipped him off." Sally took a moment to let her brilliant deduction set in.

"Unfortunately for you," she continued, "your plan didn't work, because Bones and I figured it out. And we're going to comb every inch of this place until we find the proof we need to expose you as the cruel, calculating criminal you are!"

Viola stared at Sally in disbelief, stunned, it seemed, into silence. The quiet, however, did not last long. The accused adolescent began to scream. "I am so, so, so sick of you, Sally Simplesmith! You and your stupid zombie dog! Get out of my house! Get out of my house!!"

Sally and Viola were close to blows when their parents, Officer Stu, and the D.C. arrived.

"Grwoff!" Bones warned. Sally turned her attention to the gathered grown-ups and prepared to run.

"Girls, please," Officer Stu pleaded, surveying the stand off. "Clearly there's more going on here than I know about, and I'd like to get to the bottom of it. So, why don't we call a momentary truce and—"

Before Stu could finish his proposal, a serving woman entered through a swinging door at the far end of the dining room. The D.C. lunged at Bones. The nimble corpse leapt up onto the table and raced across it, deftly navigating napkins and plates, candles and glasses.

"Bones. Kitchen!" Sally called as she sprinted toward the swinging door. The D.C. and Mrs. Vanderperfect chased after them. Terrified at the sight of the skeleton, the Vanderperfects' soon-to-be-fired maid dropped the large serving bowl of soup she had been carrying and covered her eyes. Sally and Bones cleared her before the basin hit the ground. Vivienne and the dog catcher were not so lucky. As she pushed through the kitchen door, Sally stole a quick but satisfying glance back at her pursuers, who were now covered in clam chowder.

Racing through the kitchen, she searched for an exit but saw nothing. It seemed the only way in or out was through the swinging door from which she had just escaped. Sally felt the room begin to spin. She was on the verge of passing out when a loud crash from the far corner caught her attention. Another server had just spotted

Bones and regarded him with horror. Though she had had just about enough of such narrow-minded reactions, Sally couldn't have been more thankful for this one. As she looked in the direction of the dumbfounded waiter, she spied an actual dumbwaiter. Sally whistled to Bones, who followed her into the small elevator.

"Second floor, if you know what's good for you!" she told the gaping garçon. He closed the hatch instantly and sent them upstairs.

When the dumbwaiter reached its destination, Sally threw the latch and crawled onto a landing at the end of a long hall. "I think this is the hallway where I saw Princess Poopsy. The stolen bones have to be here. Do you think you can find them?"

The dead-but-determined dog growled softly and began sniffing all around. Sally prayed that they would find what they were after. But as she threw open door after door, they uncovered nothing but overpriced furniture and more than enough portraits of Viola to fill a museum.

Sally crumpled against a door midway between the dumbwaiter and the grand staircase. "I just don't get it," she whimpered. "If it wasn't Viola, then who?"

"You, Sally Simplesmith. It must have been you," a vicious voice replied. Less than fifteen feet away stood Vivienne Vanderperfect, triumphant at the top of the stairs. Viola, the D.C., and Officer Stu were close behind. "I think it's high time you cease trying to blame someone else for your own heinous crime and simply take what's coming to you. Officer Stu, arrest them!"

"Arrest us? For what?" Sally balked.

Vivienne smiled cruelly. "Breaking and entering, fraudulence—"

"Your hideous fashion sense," Viola muttered.

"Framing me for a crime I didn't commit!" Vivienne cried.

"Wait, what?" Sally asked. "Framing *you?* Why would I frame you? Not that I did anything wrong, but why wouldn't you think I was after Viola?"

Mrs. Vanderperfect stiffened and crossed her arms. "What? Oh, well, yes, of course. Of course I meant Viola. Framing *Viola* for a crime *she* didn't commit. That's what I meant to say."

"Oh, my gosh," Sally gasped. "It wasn't Viola. It was you!"

"What was who?" Vivienne stammered. "You dare accuse me? Isn't that just...I absolutely never...Why would you even..."

Viola walked around to face her mother. "Mom? What did you do?"

Vivienne Vanderperfect looked past her daughter at Sally. She raised her perfectly manicured claws and lurched in the startled girl's direction. "I'm going to get you, you ungrateful little—!"

Sally ducked, narrowly escaping Vivienne's clutches just as Mr. Simplesmith came charging up the stairs.

"Sal—the banister!" her father hollered, and he threw himself on top of the mini-mob on the landing. Sally whistled to Bones, who leapt into her arms. Throwing her leg over the side, she straddled the banister and slid down to the ground floor.

Bones hopped onto the floor and went straight to work, sniffing out the marrowbone's pungent perfume.

"Ggruff, Ggruff!" he barked and hightailed it past the living room, through the solarium, and out to the side yard. "Rara, Ggruff," he called to Sally, who ran as fast as she could to keep up. When they reached the Vanderperfects' richly landscaped garden, Sally felt a stitch dig into her side. She didn't know how much farther she could run when Bones once again came to a sudden stop that took Sally by surprise. Tumbling over the little skeleton, she crashed into one of Mrs. Vanderperfect's oversized planters. She felt the wood split against her back and wondered how much jail time property damage would add to her sentence.

As she dug herself out of the mountain of soil that surrounded her, she was faced with a curious tableau. On the far left stood the D.C., his fists clenched as tightly as his teeth. Beside him was Officer Stu, arms crossed, frowning as he shook his head. To the right was Viola, with gaping mouth and bulging eyes, and then Sally's father, who had taken off his glasses but stared clear-eyed in his daughter's direction. Kneeling beneath them all was

Vivienne Vanderperfect, her outstretched arms paralyzed, reaching for something she would never quite grasp.

Bones trotted over to Sally and crawled into her lap. Sighing, he leaned over to her shoulder and pushed something off it with his nose. Sally heard the object land with a thud and turned to see what it was. There, in a pile of dirt, was a partially chewed marrowbone. Sally turned and beheld the broken planter behind her.

"Whoa," she whispered, as she watched mounds of soil spill out…and dozens of stolen bones fall forward.

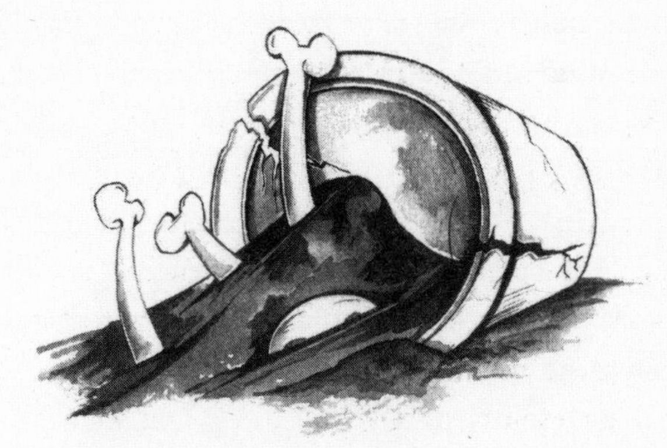

Chapter 18

TWO MONTHS, TWENTY-EIGHT DAYS, three hours, and forty-four minutes earlier, Vivienne Vanderperfect stood atop Hope Hill Cemetery, towering over her dead friend's grave. "Sorry Patty, but it's my turn now," she whispered through tightly clenched teeth. "It's my Viola shining in the spotlight, my daughter that no one will ignore. Your reign is over. Let the age of the Vanderperfects begin!" Thunder cracked, and a light rain began to fall. Vivienne laughed.

"Oh, what do you care?" She hollered to the headstones and the trees. "It's not as though you produced a worthy heir! I mean, really, Patty. Your Sally is a bit of a disappointment, wouldn't you say? I was ready for some competition, but that little freak you raised...well, let's just say I'm not quaking or shaking!"

Lightning streaked through the sky, followed by another blast of thunder.

"Not to worry, old friend," Vivienne assured. "My Vi will be a benevolent ruler, so long as your Sally stays in her place. There's plenty of room for her in the shadows." She kicked a pebble against Patty's headstone. "I should know. Thanks to you, I lived there for a very long time."

The spitting mist turned to heavy rain, and Vivienne pulled the hood of her black rain poncho over her head. "All right, all right. I can take a hint. I'll leave you to eternity. Enjoy yourself six feet under, while I finally savor the view from up top. I just wanted you to know that all those years I pretended to be your friend, all those times I stood nobly by your side are over. It's my turn now. My turn to shi—"

Out of the corner of her eye, Vivienne spied a skinny, wet figure trudging up the hill. Though she hated being interrupted in the final moments of her victory speech, she was curious to see who else would visit the cemetery on this dark and stormy night.

Slipping into the shadows of a nearby mausoleum, Vivienne watched silently as Sally Simplesmith collapsed on her mother's grave and asked for death. She witnessed lightning hit the towering oak tree above but made no move to see whether or not Sally was all right. She was about to reveal herself when a skeleton creature, risen from the dead, appeared to attack the girl, but she froze in shock when she saw actual signs of friendship develop between the terrible twosome.

Yet of all the bizarre and disconcerting things she had witnessed that night, only one event was disturbing enough to stir Vivienne to action. As Sally and Bones prepared to head home, Patty Simplesmith's pathetic daughter said the single most dangerous thing Vivienne could ever have imagined.

You're special, Vivienne heard Sally tell her foul four-legged friend. *And for the first time in my life, I think I might be special too.*

"That was when I realized Sally Simplesmith had to be stopped," Vivienne Vanderperfect now confessed. She sat in a crimson-upholstered chair at the far end of her living room as Officer Stu stood above her, jotting notes in his official police memo pad. Viola stared out the window at the dark, cold night, and the D.C. hovered uncomfortably by the door. Bones, Sally, and Seymour huddled together on a sofa across from the real bone thief.

Seymour Simplesmith had not stopped hugging his daughter or petting her dog since the family had been reunited after the discovery of Vivienne's stolen bones. As he sat listening to the confession of the woman who had framed his child, Seymour's grip tightened, and Sally had to pat his hand more than once to get him to loosen up.

"And what was it you needed to stop Sally from doing?" Officer Stu asked.

"Why from actually being special, of course," Vivienne replied brightly. "Everything was fine when she was a miserable, pathetic little nobody. Viola was the most important girl in Merryland, and that was that. But when that little monster came along and Sally stopped being so extremely depressed and uninteresting, people began to notice her more and my Vi less.

"It was the same with Patty, you know." She grimaced. "Nobody stood a chance when she was in the room. Of course, she never even noticed the effect she had. She was just so naturally charming and lovely." Vivienne shook her head. "At least in Watta City I didn't have *that* to contend with. Too bad Sally has more of her mother in her than just the eyes."

Mrs. Vanderperfect gestured for Stu to come closer, as if confiding in a sympathetic friend. "I tried sending Sally anonymous threatening notes, assuming she would have enough sense to keep her playmate under wraps, but I guess she's not as bright as her father."

Seymour's body tensed, and Sally leaned into him, hoping he would remain calm.

"By the time the girls went to the Tone Death concert, the problem had gotten quite serious. That Sally stole all Viola's friends. Had them over to her house with promises of bootleg CDs and dead dog diversions—all of them except my poor Vi."

Vivienne stared in her daughter's direction but seemed to look right through her. She did not see Viola at all. "It's a good thing I'd already taken action," she continued.

"Immediately following Viola's ruined birthday party, I called the pound and reported a perfectly crafted crime for which there could only be one suspect. And when I ran into Seymour at the concert, it didn't take much to get him to spill all the Simplesmith's secrets. He even told me about the abandoned shed at school! That's how I knew where to plant the evidence."

Mr. Simplesmith looked at his daughter, shamefaced. Sally squeezed his hand to let him know it was all right.

"Of course, it was rather unpleasant, sneaking about in the middle of night, stealing already-chewed, sometimes even buried, animal bones," Vivienne admitted. "But what other choice did I have? The way that little scene-stealer turned my elegant soiree into a three-ring circus, well, I determined to put an end to her right there."

Sally shuddered as Vivienne snapped her head in the Simplesmiths' direction. "How could you, Sally? After I took pity on you, primed you to be Viola's second-in-command? It was more than someone like you could ever have hoped for, more than you deserved. But no. You had to be different, unique, your own girl. Well, good luck with that, honey," Mrs. Vanderperfect snorted. "If it wasn't me this time, it'll be someone else the next. Someone will kill that spirit in you soon enough. You just wait and see. Your day will come, Sally Simplesmith. Your day will soon be—"

"That's enough," a voice sighed from the corner. Sally knew it well; soft and lilting, pretty and singsong, even when it said some of the cruelest things on earth. But here, now, Viola Vanderperfect's sweet soprano was sad and tired. Sally beheld her former nemesis as she approached her mother.

"What was that?" Mrs. Vanderperfect asked.

"I said, you've done enough, Mom. Let's forget about the Simplesmiths and just be the Vanderperfects." Viola kneeled at her mother's feet. "Nobody defines us, we make the rules, isn't that what you always say? So let's not worry about anyone else anymore. Let it go. Please? For me?"

Mrs. Vanderperfect cupped Viola's face in her hands. She leaned down as though about to kiss her daughter on the cheek, but she moved her lips to her ear instead. In a hissing whisper, she said, "For you? But I did this all for you. All of it. I can't believe this is the thanks I get."

Disgusted, Vivienne tossed her daughter aside. Viola lost her balance and fell to the floor. "After everything I've put into you: the ballet classes, the etiquette lessons, the clothing allowance, the personal trainer. After all I've done to make you: as perfect as you can be, to see you accept quiet defeat at the hands of a freak-show nobody like Sally Simplesmith—well, it gets me right here, kid. It gets me right here." Vivienne beat her breast as Viola gaped at her mother. "Oh, close your mouth, Vi. It's unbecoming."

Mrs. Vanderperfect rose to her feet and paced the room. "We already moved once because you couldn't hack it. Always first runner up, never top prize. You floundered in the big pond, so I thought giving you a smaller one might fix things; that you'd finally become the great white shark I had always wanted."

Vivienne glared at her child. "I guess I was wrong. You'll never be anything but a guppy."

"All right, Mrs. Vanderperfect," Officer Stu interjected uneasily. "I think we might be getting off track here. Why don't you and our dog-catching friend go into the kitchen, and we'll work out the details of how you're going to repay the town for the missing bones." He motioned to the couch on which the Simplesmiths sat. "As for how you're going to make this up to Sally—"

"Make what up to whom?" Vivienne hooted. "This is all her fault, or haven't you been listening? Well, her fault and Viola's. If you think I'll ever..."

As Mrs. Vanderperfect geared up for another spectacular rant, Sally focused on Viola, who was slowly crossing the living room. She resumed her post by the window, once again staring blankly into the night sky.

"I don't want anything," Sally said abruptly. Mrs. Vanderperfect glared at the girl who had interrupted her. "I mean, I don't want anything except Bones's and my names cleared. Other than that, I just want to go home."

"Sally, are you sure?" asked Officer Stu.

She nodded.

"Well, then, how about a nice cup of tea, Mrs. Vanderperfect? And no, that's not a request."

Vivienne made her displeasure known with a loud huff but exited the living room nonetheless. Officer Stu and the D.C. followed close behind. Sally's father gathered his things and held out his hand. "Sal? You ready to go?"

Sally looked at Viola, the girl who she had so long feared. She expected her to say something, but what did Sally want to hear? She didn't know, and Viola never said a word. She just continued staring silently out the window.

Sally turned to her father and smiled. "Yeah, Dad. I'm ready."

Taking Seymour's hand, she scooped up Bones with her other arm. The canine corpse nestled into Sally's shoulder and softly kissed her neck. When they were halfway down the drive, Sally looked back at the house and found the living room window at which Viola had sat. No one was there.

"I'm sorry," she whispered to the empty, black night.

Chapter 19

"And then, he just came back to life. I'm not kidding, Patty. We were sure Lance was a goner but, poof, there he was, flying around and nibbling on an apple core like he hadn't just flown into a lightning trap." Seymour Simplesmith kneeled beside his wife's grave. His daughter leaned on a nearby headstone, and her skeleton dog sunned himself at her feet.

"Come on, Dad. It's three o'clock already. The hot dog guy is usually gone by three fifteen, and I have to be at Chati's for dinner at seven," Sally said impatiently.

"All right, all right," her father conceded. "I just wanted to make sure your mom was up to date on everything at the lab."

"Well, if you've forgotten anything, which I highly doubt, you can tell her next week. Trust me," Sally deadpanned. "She's not going anywhere."

"Har har, Sal," Mr. Simplesmith teased. "It's just that I've got a few years of missed visits to make up for. I've a lot to get in."

Sally took her father's hand and held it tightly.

He squeezed back. "Blow your mom a kiss and let's go."

Sally did as she was told and then watched her father do the same. "See you soon, Patty," he whispered. "We love you."

"Love you, Mom!" Sally added. She touched her finger to her nose and then placed it on her mother's mended headstone. Smiling, she skipped out of the cemetery.

"GGGgggruff!" Bones added as he raced to catch up.

The Simplesmith family walked down Hope Hill toward Lazarus Park, as had become their custom on recent Sundays. When they reached Shepherd's Green, it was packed with families picnicking, kids throwing Frisbees, and more than one pickup game of hacky sack.

"Dad, over there," Sally said and pointed at an empty patch of grass under a dogwood tree.

"Why don't you put down the blanket, and I'll grab the grub. Ketchup and sauerkraut?" Her father asked.

"Don't forget the mustard," Sally added. "I want mustard too."

"You've got it, kiddo." Mr. Simplesmith winked at his daughter before jogging off to find the vendor.

Sally and Bones claimed their spot under the dogwood and spread out their blanket; Bones held one corner in his teeth while Sally fluffed and smoothed the other three. Though the tree provided little shade, Sally was more than happy to bask in the sunshine that was reflective of her current mood.

"It's funny, Bones," she said to her devoted pup as he snuggled next to her. "I always thought of myself as more of a winter or fall kind of girl. But there's something to this spring thing. It certainly makes visiting the cemetery a bit more lively."

Sally chuckled at her own joke, but Bones ignored her. He walked to the edge of the blanket and began to growl. "Geesh. This is some of my best material here. Give a girl a—"

"Grwof," Bones said quietly as he gestured with his snout toward the far end of the green. There was the D.C., standing alongside his blindingly white van, barking orders at a worker who was hunched over, picking something up from the ground.

"Hey," said Sally. "Is that—" she gasped and covered her mouth. The D.C.'s worker bee was none other than Vivienne Vanderperfect. "And it looks like she's on pooper-scooper duty! Barf!"

Bones panted, while Sally tried very hard not to laugh. "We really should be more forgiving, Bones," she scolded. "We should not revel in someone else's misfortune."

Bones closed his mouth and drooped his ears. He looked at Sally, ashamed.

"Starting tomorrow, that is." She giggled and threw her arms out for her puppy. He leapt into them with staggering force and knocked Sally on her back.

The pair was still laughing when a wayward Frisbee sailed onto their blanket. Bones scooped it up in his mouth and dropped his chest and front paws to the ground. He stuck his backside high in the air and wagged his tail furiously.

"Nice downward dog," an approaching voice trilled. Sally jumped up to receive their visitor.

"Oh, um, sorry about that, Viola," she said, sounding more nervous than she would have liked. "That's the universal dog sign for 'let's play.'"

"Princess Poopsy does the same thing," Viola offered.

"Cool," said Sally. Both girls looked awkwardly around the green. Sally accidentally glanced at the sun. She winced and stumbled a couple of steps to her left.

"Are you all right?" Viola asked, reaching out an arm to help.

"Yeah. Just stupidly blinded myself," Sally laughed as she regained her balance.

"I've done that before," Viola admitted, crossing her arms behind her back.

"Huh," Sally replied. She couldn't think of what to say next.

Bones regarded the painfully mute girls. He growled to let them know he was beginning to get bored.

"Oh, right." Sally snapped to. "Bones, give Viola back her Frisbee."

"Grwof," he replied, still holding the toy tightly in his mouth. He wiggled his high butt.

"Bones, come on," Sally commanded, but when she

moved toward him, her disobedient dog darted just beyond her reach. "Awesome," Sally sighed. Viola laughed and kneeled on the blanket.

"Bones, I know we've had our differences in the past, but may I please have the Frisbee back?" she asked, not unkindly. "You see it's not actually mine, but the people I was playing with were too scared to come over and ask for it themselves."

Bones moved from playful stance to a sit. His ears drooped and he wrinkled his brow.

"I agree. They're pretty lame," Viola told him. "So if you want to keep the Frisbee, be my guest." She glanced at Sally, who hovered above them. "But, if you want to give it back and show those dorks that you're a pretty classy little guy and that they're the weird ones, I'd be down with that too. The choice is yours."

Bones looked to Sally, who nodded. He dropped the Frisbee. Viola picked it up and fearlessly stroked the top of his head. "Thanks, Bones," she said and stood to face Sally.

"So, bye," Viola said. She half waved, then played with her hair instead.

"Yeah. See ya," said Sally. She smiled as Viola walked away.

Plopping down on the blanket, Sally leaned against the dogwood tree. She crossed her legs, and Bones crawled into her lap.

Nearby there was a sudden commotion, followed by the frightened cries of a young child. "Help!" a little boy wailed from a picnic bench. "My mommy's been stolen!"

Sally and Bones looked at each other. Though they had not discussed making a habit of their detective work, they were both quite proud of how well their first case had turned out. In silent agreement, they turned in the direction of the crying child, ready to offer their services. But when they looked again, they saw that he was already wrapped in his found mother's embrace.

"Maybe next time," Sally said.

"Grruff," Bones agreed as he settled back into her lap.

Closing her eyes, Sally inhaled deeply. When she opened them again, Bones was looking up at her. Grinning at her dead dog, she leaned in and wiggled her nose against his snout.

Together, they watched the people of Merryland enjoy a bright, sunny Sunday. Sally felt Bones's tail wag like a metronome in her lap. Her cheeks began to hurt from the wide smile that was etched on her face, but it was nothing to complain about. It was the type of pain she was happy to live with.

Acknowledgments

I've been very fortunate to have a good number of talented, generous people give their time and energy to *Sally's Bones*. Many thanks…

To Nicole James, the very best agent a girl could ask for. Your hand-holding, straight talk, and unflagging support is as appreciated as the home you found for *Sally*.

To my fantastic editor and fellow dog-lover Rebecca Frazer, whose storytelling insight brought *Sally* to a whole new level; and to the terrific team at Sourcebooks Jabberwocky, especially Kelly Barrales-Saylor, Kristin Zelazko, and Aubrey Poole. Thank you all for giving so much of yourselves to this book.

To the brilliant T.S. Spookytooth for his incredible illustrations—I am in awe of your superpowers.

To an exceptional group of writers and artists who, from the start, were my most trusted critics and tireless cheerleaders: Heather Upton, Stefanie Pintoff, Alison Sheehy, Susan Ludwig, and Doreen Marts. And to Jim McCann for coming up with the tagline, which still makes me smile!!

To my mentors, Kimberly Benston, Sue Benston, and Joe Quesada, who taught me about storytelling in its many forms.

To Jim Casey, Joe Fumarola, and the Crew for keeping me honest and making sure I didn't slack off.

To my amazing parents, Julie and Ian Cadenhead, and to my family and friends for simply being the best.

Above all, thank you to my partner in crime, Dan Buckley; my bun in the oven; and my puppy/muse, Smudge. Respectively, you believed in me always, whether I did or not; you let up on the nausea when it was time to revise; and your adorable antics inspired this story in the first place. With you three, I hit the jackpot.

About the Author

MacKenzie Cadenhead & Smudge

MacKenzie Cadenhead is a former dramaturge and was an editor for Marvel Comics. She lives in New York with her family, Dan, Phinn, and Smudge.